Planet of Joy

Charles Mills

REVIEW AND HERALD® PUBLISHING ASSOCIATION
HAGERSTOWN, MD 21740

This book was
Edited by Gerald Wheeler
Designed by Willie Duke
Electronic makeup by Shirley M. Bolivar
Cover illustration by Joe Van Severen
Typeset: 12/14 New Century Schoolbook

PRINTED IN U.S.A.

03 02 01 00 99   5 4 3 2 1

R&H Cataloging Service
Mills, Charles Henning, 1950-
    Planet of joy.

    I. Title.
                813.54

ISBN 0-8280-1359-4

Dedication

To Dorinda,
The joy of my life,
the wings of my dreams.
I love you.

The Shadow Creek Ranch Series

One Wedding and a Duck

Wendy Hanson tried to decide if anything in the world could possibly be more uncomfortable. She pulled on it, yanked on it, tried her best to ignore it, squirmed around in it, and finally decided that, even though there was a yardful of people staring at her, she was going to get out of it once and for all.

Walking stiff-legged and determined, she stumbled up the broad steps of the Station and burst through the front door just as her sister exited the den.

"Wendy? Where do you think you're going?" the older girl asked, as if she already knew the answer.

Wendy paused at the base of the curving staircase and turned to face her sibling, trying to look pleasant. "Well, hello, Debbie," she said sweetly. "Hey, nice wedding dress. You look like an angel. Gotta go."

"Gotta go?" Debbie asked, edging in her direction. "Go where?"

"To my room."

"To do what?"

Wendy frowned. "To spray paint a car."

The older girl eyed her 12-year-old sister suspiciously. "You wouldn't be thinking of changing your clothes, would you?"

"Who me? Change out of this? Why, I like this noisy, scratchy, cuts-off-my-circulation, makes-me-look-like-a-pumpkin dress. Whatever would cause you to think that I wanted to do such a totally insane thing?"

Debbie gathered the billowing folds of her wedding dress with one arm while trying to follow her sister up to the second floor. "You can't change now. The ceremony is about to begin. Grandpa just got back, and Samantha says Pastor Webley is beginning to clear his throat."

"I don't care," Wendy shot back over her shoulder. "I feel like an apple dumpling in this stupid dress. I'm going to put my jeans and sweatshirt on before I explode." She paused at her bedroom door. "I'm going to put on my riding boots too. So *live* with it!"

Debbie grabbed her sister's arm with her free hand. "Please, Wendy. Do I ever ask you to do anything for me?"

"Every minute of every day."

The older girl nodded. "Yes, but have I ever asked you to wear a dress before?"

"No. And now I know why."

6

The older girl groaned in frustration. "Wendy Hanson, you just can't change now. You'll spoil my wedding. What will people think if they see you standing by the guest book or sitting on the front row looking like . . . like . . . Lewis and Clark?"

"*They* can live with it, too!"

As the girls stumbled into the room, Wendy already had her dress down around her ankles and was reaching for the pair of soiled and faded blue jeans draped over the end of her bed.

"Wait . . . wait!" Debbie pleaded, trying to come up with some sort of enticement to stop the half-undressed girl from transforming herself from sister of the bride to wilderness explorer. "If you do this for me, I'll never ask another favor from you for the rest of your life."

"Never?" Wendy said, leg paused in midair, pants positioned below the heel.

"Never. I may want you to do something so bad it makes my teeth itch, but I won't ask. I'll just do it myself."

The younger girl turned. "Does that include washing dishes and cleaning your bathroom that smells like a perfume factory?"

"Yes."

"Does that include taking messages for you from your boring business friends in Bozeman who call you all the time wanting you to do stuff out at the mall and I can never find you 'cause you're out dancing around in the pasture with Barry Gordon?"

"That too."

Wendy thought for a minute. "Do you . . . do you promise to go riding with me every once in a while even though Barry wants you to do something with him?"

A gentle smile began to soften Debbie's worried face. "Yes, if that would make you happy."

"And do you promise to talk to me like in the past when I needed to know about girl stuff and Dad got all embarrassed?"

"Yes."

Relaxing, Wendy lowered herself onto the bed. "And do you promise that you will forever and ever and ever be . . . my sister even though you're getting married and moving up to Papoose Lake where Barry is building you a house with a porch on it?"

Debbie sat down beside her. "I will always be your sister, and you are always welcome to come up to my house and sit on my porch and we can talk about anything you want."

"Including boys?"

The older girl blinked. "Boys? You want to know about boys?"

Wendy shrugged. "Hey, you never know. I'm becoming a young lady—at least that's what Dad says—and young ladies sometimes have to do crazy things like go out on dates with boys, although I don't see what the great attraction is."

Her sister nodded. "Yes. We can talk about boys, or anything else." She paused. "So will you wear the dress just a little longer, at least until after the ceremony? Then you can put on whatever you want for the reception."

"Can I wear my ranch hat?"

"If that will make you more comfortable."

With a sigh Wendy reached for the pink and white folds of cloth billowing about her ankles. "When I get married," she said, "everyone can wear whatever they want, *including* jeans and sweatshirts. They can even wear a bathing suit if they choose to."

"Fair enough," Debbie said, helping the younger girl readjust the waistband and smooth the twisted sleeves. Running gentle fingers through her sister's short, blond hair, she added, "There, you look beautiful—even in this dress."

Wendy nodded shyly. "And . . . you look beautiful too, Debbie. Even in this . . . this long white thing."

The older girl smiled. "Thanks, sister."

Leaning over, Wendy hugged the bride. "You're welcome . . . sister. Now, let's go out and do this thing before I get scratched to death and you have to call the paramedics."

Hand in hand the two left the bedroom and made their way down the long staircase and across the foyer. From outside, soft guitar and organ music drifted in the cool autumn air. Across the lawn, by the footbridge, Pastor Webley stood next to Barry Gordon, still clearing his throat.

Seven-year-old Samantha sat on a folding chair near the front of the gathering with Lizzy Pierce on one side and Grandma and Grandpa Hanson on the other. Behind them in neat rows ranged the other wedding guests, each with smiles lighting their faces, expectantly waiting for the bride to appear on the broad front porch of the Station situated behind them, beyond the smooth, carefully clipped lawn. Heads turned while whispers mingled with the sweet scent of the roses lining the center aisle separating the friends of the bride from the friends of the groom.

"I see Wendy," Samantha announced, pointing at the young girl who quickly descended the steps and walked, somewhat awkwardly, over to where Mrs. Webley, the minister's wife, sat pumping the pedals and tapping the keys of an old organ. The girl in the pink and white dress leaned close to the musician and whispered something in her ear. The music stopped. The guitarist put down his instrument, and the organist joined her fingers in front of her and cracked her knuckles with a resounding *snap*. Then, after pumping furiously to build up pressure in the old organ, she lowered her hands until they hovered just over the keys. Finally, with a determined flourish, she pounced on the keyboard, sending the familiar chords of the wedding march out across the gathering and over the horse pasture beyond the footbridge.

All eyes turned to stare back at the Station, while Barry Gordon suddenly found it hard to swallow. There, standing at the top of the broad steps, white gown glowing brightly in the early afternoon sun, stood Debbie, a thin, wispy veil covering the soft flush of her face. A train of lacy fabric cascaded past the dark folds of her perfectly arranged hair, slipped by her shoulders, and flowed to the floor before forming silken waves that washed out behind her. Across the crown of the veil was a row of delicate wildflowers, and in her hands she held a bouquet of yellow daisies.

So impressive was her image at the top of the stairs that everyone's breath caught in their throats, sending an absolute silence out over the lawn. Even Mrs. Webley's fingers froze in midchord, her eyes unable to tear themselves away from the young woman waiting at the top of the stairs.

Lizzy Pierce leaned down and spoke softly into Samantha's ear. "That's your cue, sweetheart," she said.

Samantha nodded, then glanced at the basket nestled in her lap. "Oh yes. *Oh yes!*" the little dark-skinned girl breathed, stumbling to her feet. Still staring at the beautiful bride at the top of the distant steps, she made her way to the end of the long carpeted aisle and stopped at her assigned post, waiting for her signal to start spreading rose petals down the aisle between the two groups of guests.

Mrs. Webley, suddenly realizing that the music had stopped, attacked the keys with an even greater sense of determination, sending the soaring chords out across the gathering once again. Dressed in a dark suit and tie, Mr. Hanson appeared next to his daughter, and Debbie slipped her hand around the curve of his arm. Slowly, carefully, they descended the steps and made their way toward the seated assembly. As they crossed the lawn, young ranchhand Joey Dugan and much-loved neighbor Merrilee Dawson took up positions behind Samantha and, following the little girl's lead, walked along the rose-bordered aisle until they arrived at the base of the footbridge. Once there, they stood beside the minister and groom, waiting for the bride to make her way toward them.

Barry found unexpected tears welling up in his eyes. How he loved Debbie! And to think that she would love him enough to agree to be his wife was more than he could comprehend. It was here by the footbridge that he had discovered for the first time that he was in love with her.

He remembered the day she'd shyly tried to catch his attention and they'd both ended up falling into the very cold and very wet waters of Shadow Creek. It was here above the moon-sparkled waves that they'd first spoken intimate whispers of commitment and affection to each other. And now, it was here that they'd join their lives forever with the blessing of God and approval of family and friends. Theirs had been a courtship of mutual growth and restrained passion. It had been a relationship built on the dreams of the future, not on the desires of the present. Each knew that he or she could trust the other, come what may, to remain faithful and true to promises they'd be sharing that day.

As the grand chords of the old pump organ filled the valley, Barry Gordon knew that he'd found the girl of his dreams and that he would love her until the day he died.

Debbie stepped forward, supported by the arm of her father. She smiled, holding back tears of her own. It was her day, her time, her moment. And it was perfect.

❖ ❖ ❖

Tugging gently on the reins, Wendy slowed her horse to a walk, allowing the warm sun to soak into their faces as they clippety-clopped along the mountaintop trail. It was midday in late October. The wedding and its scratchy, uncomfortable dress were only fading memories now, replaced by new challenges, new problems to endure, the latest of which weighed heavily on the young girl's mind.

"Let's stop and rest for a minute," Wendy suggested, guiding her horse Early toward a fallen log lying at the edge of a high meadow. The animal snorted softly as if to say, "Rest? *You* need rest? Just who's been climbing these mountains all morning, anyway?"

The girl slipped from the saddle and landed with a muffled plop on the short, dry grass that just a few weeks before had been thick with summer growth. Repeated nights of heavy frost had turned the meadow carpet into straw. Early ambled a short distance away in search of something to munch on while his young rider settled with a sigh on the log.

"Now what am I supposed to do?" he heard her say. "Everything's changing and I can't stop it." He saw her kick at a piece of rotting bark. "Just when life's going pretty good, along comes something that messes it all up. Man, being 12 is the pits!"

Early sampled some still-green growth hiding behind a large boulder and decided to let Wendy work out without his assistance whatever problem was making her so grumpy. After all, he'd been working hard, carrying her halfway around Montana since they'd left the Station after breakfast. He deserved a little peace and quiet . . . and a snack. She'd just have to figure things out by herself.

Wendy watched a hawk glide effortlessly in the clear blue sky overhead. How often she'd wished she could fly on powerful wings, rising high above the earth with its pain and troubles like a bird riding mountain thermals. But she was a person, not a hawk. She was also a 12-year-old sixth grader who lived on a beautiful ranch with a loving family and had her very own horse to ride. But even all of those blessings weren't enough to keep problems from plaguing her, spoiling her fun, making her work harder at happiness than she thought necessary.

The latest attack on her contentment had come just yesterday, at breakfast, when her father raised his hand, indicating that he had an important announcement to make.

"We got a phone call from New York last night," he said after everyone had either stopped talking or stuffed enough oatmeal into their mouths to make speech difficult. "Seems Lizzy's sister is ailing and needs someone to care for her right away. I've arranged for Mrs. Pierce to fly back on Sunday. We hope this will be only a temporary situation, but illnesses like these can be tricky. In any case, we'll miss our good friend and home school teacher very much."

All eyes had turned to the end of the table where Lizzy Pierce sat looking anything but pleased with the latest turn of events. "I'll miss you all so much," she said softly. "But Sissy needs me, and I'm the only one left in the family who can care for her. She lives alone out on Long Island, and if I don't go, she'll suffer more than she needs to."

"We understand," Mr. Hanson stated, deep sympathy filling his voice. "You just go and do what you need to do, and we'll muddle on without you until you get back. Don't you worry about us, OK?"

Lizzy nodded, then glanced at Wendy. "I . . . I won't be able to be your teacher this year for home school, and your father and I have decided that perhaps you should attend the local public school until I get back. Joey's busy with his freshman studies at Bozeman State three days a week, and Grandma Hanson has volunteered to help Samantha with her courses. But you, Wendy dear, would need someone to keep you motivated. School work isn't exactly your favorite activity, right?"

Wendy grinned. "I'd rather hike in the mountains, if that's what you mean."

"Exactly," Lizzy responded with a smile. "So we figured you could use a firm hand to keep you on track educationally."

Joey leaned forward. "That's a nice way of saying that without someone to ride your case, you'd flunk everything but recess."

Lizzy shook her head. "You see, Wendy, school is supposed to teach you more than facts, figures, and history dates. Whether you attend classes at a public facility or do your lessons in the Station den beside the hearth, you're learning self-discipline, keeping schedules, meeting challenges, and seeing projects through to the end. That's what life is all about, especially when you get older."

Samantha waved her hand. "If Lizzy isn't here

and Grandma Hanson is my teacher, do I still have to learn how to add three numbers?"

"Yes," the old woman beside her said lovingly, adding a hug to her response. "And multiply and divide and subtract them, too."

The little girl sighed and looked up at her adopted grandmother. "If I have to do too many problems like that, I'll get as sick as Lizzy's sister."

Wendy frowned. "I don't want to go to public school." Then she brightened. "Tell you what, I'll study harder here at home. Honest. I'll read every assignment and look up stuff on the Internet and even finish that report on . . . on . . ."

"South America?" Lizzy prompted.

"Yeah, South America. I'll even get it in on time. When's it due—tomorrow, Friday?"

"Two weeks ago," the woman sighed, with a knowing grin.

Wendy blinked. "Well, what about that science experiment where I'm supposed to grow a seed in a jar with only water and no dirt?"

"*That's* due tomorrow."

The girl glanced about the table in sudden desperation. "Anybody here have any fast-growing seeds on you?"

Lizzy shook her head. "You're a very smart girl, Wendy," she said with pride. "It makes you able to do anything you want without even breaking a sweat. But it's just that you need someone to keep you in those books, someone to make sure

17

you complete your assignments. Grandma Hanson says that with me gone, housework will take up too much of her time. Samantha will be all she can handle. I'm sorry, Wendy. We don't have any other choice."

"Any other choice," the girl repeated as the hawk disappeared behind a distant mountain. "Great. Now I've got to go to school with a bunch of morons who'll probably hate me and call me things like Pyrite Head." She fingered the unruly golden strands of hair sticking out from under her favorite ranch hat. "And I'll have to wear clean clothes and everything. Every day! Man, life is the *pits!*"

The hawk reappeared and floated down through the valley that spread toward the east. Mount Blackmore rose stately and proud beyond, its snow-covered 10,000-foot summit crowning the boundaries of the Gallatin National Forest. Wendy had attended public school for several years back in New York City. Not having liked it then, she knew beyond a shadow of a doubt she wouldn't like it now.

It wasn't that she hated learning—it was just that she liked to learn at her own pace, on her own schedule. During the past three years Lizzy had accepted her rather unorthodox study habits and worked around them. Wendy did get everything done—eventually. But the girl knew that public school with its stricter schedules and more exact rules would blow her learning style clean out of

18

the water. Home school suited her perfectly. Going to class with a roomful of other students didn't. And, most troublesome of all, she'd be out of reach of her beloved mountains every single school day.

"Hey, Early," she called, rising on tired legs. "Come on. Let's get back to the Station. I'm getting kinda hungry myself, and this meadow grass doesn't look all that appealing." The little stallion obediently sauntered over to his master and stood patiently as she lifted herself up and settled comfortably in the saddle. "We'll have to save our rides for the weekend," she announced, as if breaking a bit of horrible news to the horse trotting below her. "But don't worry, they can take the girl out of the mountains, but they can't take the mountains out of the girl. If I have to attend school like all the other lemmings in the world, they'll just have to learn that this rodent is a force to be reckoned with." She paused. "Wait, that didn't come out quite right."

Horse and rider galloped away, catching the cool breezes off the high meadow. With a growing feeling of uncertainty, Wendy headed for the valley far below where the grand Station stood by a sparkling creek, and where 12-year-old girls had to learn that, even in Montana, life didn't always unfold to their liking. Still, she figured that if she could survive being knocked off a mountain by a stray lightning bolt, getting snowbound in a house with no heat, or being swallowed by the earth itself, she could withstand attending public school for a while. What were a bunch of kids compared to the force of Mother Nature herself?

✧ ✧ ✧

"Wendy?" a male voice called from the other side of the closed bedroom door. "Wendy, are you awake?"

"No," the girl moaned.

"Well, you'd better get awake. Grandma Hanson's got pancakes on the stove, and your dad sent me up here to find out if you're still alive."

"Go away."

"I'm supposed to take you to Gallatin Gateway this morning. It's your first day at your new school, remember? Are you nervous?"

"Why are you talking to me?"

"Besides, you get to ride in my new old truck, if it will start, although it should 'cause Grandpa Hanson put a new battery in it yesterday. That vehicle sure makes the girls' heads turn at the university."

Wendy pulled the covers up over her ears. "They're trying to figure out what idiot would buy something that looks like the Montana Air National Guard used it for bombing practice."

The teenager opened the door and stuck his head into the room, a smile lighting his sun-tanned face. "It just needs a little paint."

"Paint? Listen, Mr. Dugan, I don't mean to be

the bearer of bad news, but paint doesn't stick too good to rust."

Joey laughed. "You're just jealous that I've got a vehicle and all you've got is a scrawny horse."

Wendy sat up straight. "Scrawny? Early isn't scrawny. You must mean Tar Boy, that ugly collection of skin, bones, and hair you call a horse. Now, *that's* scrawny!"

"Tar Boy can outrun, outjump, outclimb, and outpull any horse on the ranch, and you know it."

"In your dreams."

"Dreams nothin'! Why, Tar Boy is the best horse in southern Montana. Even Wrangler Barry says so."

Wendy shook her head and frowned at him. "Barry has about as much horse sense as he does girl sense. I mean, look who he married!"

"Guys, guys, guys," another male voice called from the hallway. "It's too early in the morning to listen to you two get on each other's cases." Mr. Hanson's frowning face appeared at the door. "Wendy, get up! Joey, go . . . go do whatever you do out in the barn so you can help get little Miss Congeniality here and your overconfident self to your respective places of higher education on time. OK?"

"Good morning, Daddy," Wendy said, her words stretched by a wide yawn.

"Yes, sir, Mr. H," Joey called, turning to leave. "I was just trying to get her up. Now you can have the pleasure." He paused and placed an under-standing hand on the man's shoulder. "Good luck."

Mr. Hanson chuckled. "I've been doing it longer than you have and know what you mean. Thanks for the encouragement."

As Joey trotted away, the lawyer entered his daughter's bedroom and sat down at the foot of her bed. "How're you doin', sweetheart? Usually you're up long before this, wandering the halls like the ghost of Christmas past. As a matter of fact, you're usually up before the roosters crow in *Ohio.*" He smiled down at his daughter. "Are you ready for your new adventure?"

"Isn't that what Caesar said to the Christians right before he dropped them off at the Coliseum?"

"No. He told them that the lions had invited them over for dinner."

"Yuck!" Wendy winced.

Mr. Hanson smoothed the hair streaking her forehead. "It won't be all that bad. You'll see."

Wendy sighed. "I don't like crowds of people any-more," she said. "I like being alone, up in the moun-tains with Early, exploring the old logging roads every afternoon. Now, three days a week, I have to take my life in my hands and ride with Joey Dugan, and the other two days I've got to sit in a big yellow school bus with a bunch of noisy strangers."

"The logging roads will still be there on the weekends," Mr. Hanson encouraged, "and Early's not going anywhere either. It's just for a few months or a little longer. You'll do fine."

Wendy edged close to her father and settled herself in the circle of his arms. "But what if they don't like me? What if they think I'm weird?"

"You *are* weird," Mr. Hanson stated.

The girl grinned. "Yeah, well, I don't like anyone reminding me of that fact."

The man held his daughter close. "If anybody bothers you, you just tell me about it. I'll personally go over to that school and sue those little monsters for everything they own. They won't have disposable income until they're 50!"

Wendy batted her eyes. "Why, Mr. Hanson, you'd do that for little ol' me?"

"Absolutely. Now, as your lawyer it is my duty to inform you that breakfast is being served and that if you don't get out of this bed in the next three seconds, I'll get Samantha in here with Pueblo the dog, and they'll start your day in their own special way."

"I'm up, *I'm up!*" the girl giggled, jumping out of bed. "Just keep that dog and his overactive spit glands away from me."

Mr. Hanson laughed. "Deal," he said, walking to the door. He paused for a moment and studied the pajama-clad form of his daughter. "I love you, Wendy," he said softly. "And I know that the Lewis and Clark Elementary School will be a terrific place for you to learn. Says so in the brochure."

Wendy narrowed her eyes. "I'm sending a jar of

vitamins to Lizzy's sister so she'll get better *fast*— just in case."

With that she grabbed her cleanest pair of blue jeans, pulled her favorite red sweatshirt down from a closet hook, and headed for the bathroom door. Before turning to leave, Mr. Hanson noticed something unusual in the now empty room. Wendy's riding boots, the pair she wore most, had been shined. A Station first.

Joey shifted and released the clutch, causing the vehicle to slow slightly as it rounded a curve. Wendy studied the somewhat mismatched dials and engine instruments fronting the cab of the little foreign truck and shook her head in disbelief. "And you paid how much for this pile of junk?"

Joey grinned proudly. "$500."

The girl ran her fingers along the top of the dashboard, inspecting a long gash. "Boy, they saw *you* coming."

"Hey," the driver said, "this is a great truck. Engine works—most of the time. It's got good tires, and the brakes are only a year old. Grandpa Hanson showed me how to adjust them myself. Besides, Wrangler Barry taught me how to drive, remember? He said my skills behind the wheel were—how did he put it?—beyond description."

Wendy chuckled. "And I suppose you took that as a compliment?"

Joey frowned. "Well, yeah. Wasn't it?"

The girl smiled. "Sure, Joey. You're a natural."

The truck slammed into a deep rut and bounced out again. Joey glanced at his passenger and cleared his throat. "I'll bet you didn't think I saw that one, huh? Well, I just wanted to show you how strong this ol' vehicle is." He patted the steering wheel lovingly. "Built like a tank."

"Rides like one too," Wendy moaned, rubbing the small of her back. "And to think I get to sit in this . . . this Spam can with wheels twice a day, three days a week."

"Hey," Joey responded with a frown, "you can get out and walk if you want."

Wendy shook her head. "Nah. I'd get to school way too early. Besides—*watch out!*"

Joey swerved as what looked like some type of animal appeared out of nowhere and flashed by the front of the truck. The two occupants heard a sharp *thump,* then the vehicle skidded to a dusty stop.

"You hit it. *You hit it!*" Wendy wailed.

Joey's hands began to tremble. "Yeah. I think I did. But I didn't mean to. Honest. I didn't see whatever it was until it was too late. Oh, what have I done? What have I done?"

The girl, seeing how truly shaken he was, softened a little. "It's OK, Joey. You couldn't stop in time. It was an accident."

"But I may have killed some animal with my

truck. I wasn't going fast or anything. It just shot by and I hit it."

"Really, Joey, it's OK. Maybe the animal isn't hurt bad. Maybe it just got up and ran away."

The boy slowly opened the door and looked back in the direction they'd just come. At first he couldn't see anything because of the dust. Then as the air began to clear, he noticed a small mound of feathers lying in the gravel by the road 15 to 20 feet behind them. The feathers didn't move and no sound disturbed the valley silence.

The door creaked and snapped as Joey opened it wider and stepped out of the truck. "I think it's a goose or a duck," he whispered, as if the fallen fowl were asleep and he didn't want to wake it. "Do you see it, Wendy? Do you see what I did?"

Wendy unfastened her seatbelt, slipped from the truck cab, and joined him at the rear of the vehicle. Both stood staring at the bird, afraid to think of what they'd see if they moved any closer.

"You didn't mean to," Wendy whispered. "Really, Joey. It was an accident."

Suddenly the mound of feathers shifted slightly, then became still again. "Hey," Joey breathed, "I think it moved. Didn't it move?"

Wendy shook her head. "Yeah. There, it did it again. I think it's still alive."

The two edged forward, pressed against each other for support, moving as one toward the pile of broken feathers by the side of the road. As they neared the bird they heard a faint *quack*. Then a *quack, quack*.

Joey pointed. "Dead animals don't quack, do they?"

"No," Wendy stated. "They just lie still and don't say anything."

Quack.

The boy studied the creature for a long moment. "It's alive."

"I think you're right," his companion agreed.

"Maybe we should take it someplace, you know, like to a vet."

Wendy slowly knelt beside the stricken bird and ran her hand over the rumpled feathers, some of which jutted at odd angles from the body. "I don't think any bones are broken," she said. "And there's no blood." She leaned forward and examined the creature more thoroughly, being careful not to cause any more pain. "It's a duck, a male mallard duck. See the green head and gray rump feathers? These guys fly over the Station all the time, especially in the fall. This one's kinda late. He must've been left behind when the rest of the flock headed south. Maybe he's old and can't fly all day like the others."

Joey joined her. "Will he be OK? I mean, is he going to die?"

The girl shook her head. "I don't think so. Red Stone taught me and Plenty a lot about animals and how they're strong and can live through stuff, even getting creamed by a really ugly truck."

Joey frowned. "My truck's not ugly. It has character. That's what Grandpa Hanson says."

Wendy chuckled. "This from a man who thinks primer is a fashion accessory."

"So?" the boy pressed, "will the duck be OK?"

Wendy reached down and gently lifted the bird into her arms. The animal's eyes blinked open and he stared at the young girl for a long moment, as if trying to size her up. Was she a danger to him? Or would she help him? The little duck must've decided on the latter because it slowly, painfully tucked its brown beak under a collection of dirt-stained and somewhat frayed wing feathers and went quickly to sleep.

"Yes," Wendy nodded, stumbling to her feet, duck held securely against her chest. "He'll be fine, although he's pretty badly bruised. Maybe he's got some cracked ribs and stuff. It'll be a while before he can fly again, or even walk for that matter, but our friend will live if he gets lots of care and someone brings him food to eat. Out here in the wild, the mountain lions would put him out of his misery fast."

"Should we head back to the Station?" Joey asked.

"No," Wendy sighed, glancing at her watch. "I'm going to be late to school as it is now. We've gotta go on." The two started for the truck. "I'll watch over Feathers for the rest of the day. Then we'll find a nice quiet place for him at the Station when we get home this afternoon."

Joey slipped into the driver's seat and twisted the key in the ignition. "Let me get this straight," he said. "You're going to show up at a new school filled with people you don't know while carrying a duck in your arms?"

Wendy groaned. "It's gonna look kinda strange, isn't it?"

The driver shook his head. "They'll crucify you, Wendy. They'll laugh you right out of class. Wouldn't you rather that we drop the little guy off somewhere?"

The girl smoothed the soft down covering the sleeping bird's back. "We hit 'im. We should take care of 'im. Just don't be late picking me up this afternoon. I don't wanna stand around after school for very long—if you know what I mean."

Joey guided his rattling, vibrating truck over the rutted road and glanced over at his two passengers. "I'll be there right at 3:00," he said. Then he added, "You're somethin' else, Wendy. Do you know that? You're one of a kind."

"Why, Mr. Dugan, I appreciate the compliment."

The driver blinked. "Compliment? You took that as a compliment?"

With a smile Wendy continued stroking the creature resting comfortably in her lap. The day was going to be one of a kind as well. She closed her eyes. Just how would she face a new school filled with curious eyes while holding a sleeping duck in her arms?

The old truck turned right onto State Highway 191 and headed north. Gallatin Gateway was but a few miles ahead. Whatever the day held in store, she'd just have to face it, duck and all.

CHAPTER 2

Birds of
a Feather

Joey's truck clattered away from the curb, leaving Wendy standing in front of a large brick building with tall glass windows and a row of thick pillars guarding the entrance. From her shoulders hung a backpack filled with pencils, notebooks, and a pocket calculator. In her arms she held a duck.

The structure reminded her of pictures she'd seen of elegant Southern plantations except, in this case, it had no long porches or wispy webs of Spanish moss hanging from the almost leafless trees nearby. A sidewalk curved gracefully from where she stood to a set of wide steps fronting enormous green doors. Above the entrance, in glowing yellow letters, were carved the words, "LEWIS AND CLARK ELEMENTARY SCHOOL —Teaching Tomorrow's Great Explorers Today."

"Oh great," the girl groaned to herself, looking around at the empty front lawn and silent playground off to her right. "Everyone's inside just waiting to make my day more miserable than it already is."

She glanced down at the mallard held tightly in her arms. "Are you ready for this?" she asked.

The duck wiggled its head and snorted softly as if to say, "Thirty minutes ago I got hit by a really ugly truck. I've got enough to worry about."

Drawing in a deep breath, Wendy walked up the sidewalk, climbed the steps, and pushed open one of the doors. The hallway was empty. From places unseen echoed the sounds of education as future explorers learned whatever their teachers and the state of Montana had decided was needed to prepare them for the wildernesses of life.

Wendy noticed a sign hanging above a nearby door: "Registrar." "This is where we go," she whispered. The duck didn't respond. Like all wild animals trying to heal themselves, it had fallen asleep again.

The girl opened the door and approached a woman sitting stiff and businesslike at a metal desk, typing furiously on an old, rattling typewriter. Her dark brown hair had been cropped close to her head, making her ears stick out like miniature wings. "I'll be right with you," she said without looking up.

With a few more pounding entries, she whipped the paper from the machine and held it at arm's length, examining the results of her labor through thick, silver-rimmed glasses. "You can keep your computers and fancy printers," she proclaimed to no one in particular. "Just give me a good ol' IBM Selectric and a clean piece of 20-pound and I can create correspondence anyone would be proud of." She quickly folded the letter and jammed it into an envelope. Lifting a pre-printed form from her drawer, she dropped it expertly into the typewriter, twisted it into position, and called out, "Name?"

Wendy blinked. "Ah, Wendy. Wendy Hanson."

"Oh, yes," the woman said, still not allowing her eyes to move from the machine, her fingers tapping like pistons in an engine. "You're from Shadow Creek Ranch. Your father was in here last week. Age?"

The girl cleared her throat. "Twelve. Twelve and a half. My birthday's in June."

"Everyone's in a hurry to grow up," the woman said, continuing to type. "Any special diet or scheduled medicines?"

Wendy frowned. "I'm a vegetarian, if that's what you mean."

"No animal products." The registrar spoke the words as she typed them. "Any allergies?"

"I think homework gives me a rash."

The woman didn't flinch. "No reported allergies," she typed-spoke. "Money?"

The girl smiled. "Sure, I'll take some."

The registrar's fingers paused for a split second. "I meant, do you have money on you to pay meal or lab fees, but I take it you don't. I'm glad you find our school admissions form humorous. You can laugh your way clear through the sixth grade if you like." She lifted the paper from the typewriter and expertly thrust it into an open file drawer at her knee. Then she rose and hurried across the room, calling over her shoulder. "You're in room 1-F. Teacher's Miss Elrod. And you're late. First class has already begun. Welcome to Lewis and Clark."

Wendy watched the woman busy herself at a tall file cabinet. "Thanks," she said.

The registrar responded with a melodious, "You're laaa-ate."

"Yeah. 1-F. I'm outta here. See ya."

She saw the woman wave without turning, then dig into some papers, mumbling something about how her work was never done and completely unappreciated.

Back in the hallway, Wendy studied the room numbers and letters screwed tightly into the doors. 1-C, 1-D, 1-F. "Here we are," she said, trying to sound hopeful. "I wonder what Miss Elrod is like."

The door burst open, startling her as a boy her age exited the classroom. He glanced at Wendy and the duck. "Weird," he said, then hurried down the hall toward a door emblazoned with the silhouette figure of a man.

"Is someone out there?" Wendy heard a woman's

voice call. Stepping through the doorway, she found herself standing at the front of a large room filled with students, all staring at her in complete and utter silence. The teacher stood by the blackboard, hand poised in midword, fingers dusted white with chalk. "May I help you?" she asked.

Wendy shifted her position. "Ah, yes ma'am. My name is Wendy Hanson, and I'm supposed to be your student." The girl suddenly discovered that all the saliva in her mouth had vanished, leaving her tongue feeling as if it was lying on a bed of desert sand.

Miss Elrod's eyes narrowed slightly, giving her otherwise friendly face a somewhat tense look. "My dear, are you aware that you're holding a duck in your arms?"

"Yes, ma'am," Wendy breathed, her knees trembling. "You see, Joey—that's the guy who takes care of the horses on the ranch—hit him with his truck, and I'm trying to make him well again. We couldn't just leave him by the road, and we were late already, so I decided I'd bring him to school with me . . . if that's OK. He won't bother anyone."

Just then the duck raised its head and let out a loud *QUACK!*

The room erupted into laughter as Wendy's face glowed crimson. Miss Elrod immediately called for silence and walked over to where her new pupil stood. Her movements were graceful and professional, an easy match to her carefully ironed dress and polished shoes. Every strand of her auburn hair was in place, held tightly by a set of small matching combs. "Will you be bringing wild animals to school every day?" she asked.

"No, ma'am. Only those that Joey hits with his truck."

Laughter burst throughout the room again. This time Miss Elrod's rosy lips quivered slightly in a suppressed grin. "That will be fine. Now take your place in that empty seat over by the window, and we'll find a nice, comfortable box in which to place your feathered friend for the day." She paused. "Does he have a name?"

"Well," Wendy said, edging to her spot by the large expanse of glass, "Joey and I kinda call him Feathers 'cause he's got a lot of 'em."

Miss Elrod nodded. "Well, put Feathers in that box over there by the bookcase and cover him with something so he can rest. We'll talk about this more later, OK?"

"OK," Wendy whispered. She'd never been so embarrassed in all her life. Her world during the past few years had been cozy dens and wide-open spaces high atop endless mountain ranges. Now, here she was, jammed into a classroom with dozens her age who must be thinking that she was the weirdest individual ever to walk the earth.

Eyes followed her every movement. Giggles hissed through fingers held tightly against mouths as she lowered the injured duck into an empty box and covered it with an open newspaper. Then she took her seat and folded her hands in front of her, not looking to the left or to the right. Her greatest desire at that moment was for the ground to open up below her and allow her to fall into its inky darkness.

"Welcome, Wendy," Miss Elrod said with a genuine, but cautious smile. "We're studying geography during our first session this morning. Your textbook is under your seat. Please open to page 69."

As Wendy bent to retrieve the assigned book, she heard someone behind her quack softly. Then a student across the room did the same, followed by several other renditions of what the young mimics believed was a reasonable imitation of duck talk. The girl closed her eyes. Yup. This was about what she'd expected her day to be like. Glancing at the big clock above the blackboard, she took note that she'd been at the Lewis and Clark school for exactly 18 minutes. Only six hours and 42 minutes to go.

"We're studying South America," Miss Elrod announced for the new student's benefit. "Can anyone list five of its countries?"

Sighing, Wendy shook her head. South America was proving to be an extremely persistent continent in her life.

✧ ✧ ✧

The noon hour provided some welcome relief to

the day's strangeness. Wendy gathered her lunch at the cafeteria line and hurried out into the cool late autumn air, selecting a spot at the far end of the playground to enjoy her food. At her feet was the box containing the somewhat more lively duck.

"You're lucky," Wendy said between bites of her lettuce and tomato sandwich. A steaming bowl of cream of celery soup sat on the bench beside her. "You don't have to go to school. All you need to do is fly south to some deserted beach and tan your feathers all winter." She paused. "Of course, you've got to dodge hunters' bullets, keep an eye open for hungry hawks, stay out of reach of snapping turtles while swimming in ponds, and fly above truck level, especially over roads. H'mmm. I guess we both have our problems."

The duck's head tilted slightly as he watched the girl with the short blond hair take a bite out of her sandwich. Wendy noticed the careful scrutiny she was receiving from her web-footed friend and grinned broadly. "You're hungry, aren't you? That's great. That means you're not hurt too bad inside. Red Stone, my old Indian friend who used to spend his summers up on Freedom Mountain, taught me and his granddaughter Plenty that if an animal or person is hungry after an injury, that's a good sign. Healing takes energy. Energy comes from food. So . . ." Wendy pulled out a fat chunk of lettuce and dangled it in front of the duck. "How would you like a piece of—"

In an instant the big green leaf vanished.

"Wow!" Wendy breathed. "You *are* hungry." She extracted another portion from her bulging sandwich. Feathers downed that offering too, his beak smacking in jubilant ecstasy. "This is good. This is very good," she said, watching her small companion eagerly take the food she offered. "You'll be well and flyin' south in no time."

"I like your duck," a voice said. Wendy glanced up to see a girl standing some distance away, as if too shy to approach any farther.

"Well, at least he likes lettuce," she said. "'Cept I'm about to run out."

"Here," the stranger called, lifting her tray of food. "He can have some of mine."

Wendy watched her visitor walk slowly, almost methodically, toward her. The girl's faded jacket and much-worn pants hung from her bony arms and legs like flags without a wind. Her face appeared etched with frown lines, and dark shadows hung under her slightly puffy eyes. Her hair was thin and wayward. "I'm really not hungry. Feathers can have as much as he likes."

With a smile Wendy made room for the girl on the bench. "Are you sure?" she asked.

"Oh yes. I don't eat much. I've been kinda sick, and food doesn't taste too good sometimes." The stranger held out a slice of apple in the duck's direction. "My name's Emily, and I sit near the back of Miss Elrod's class. Boy, you musta been embarrassed this morning, new kid in school, comin' in late, Feathers."

Wendy grinned. "I've had better days."

"Well, I for one think that what you're doing is very nice, taking care of this little guy and all. It's not fun to hurt. Believe me." She offered another morsel to the duck. "Some days I feel like a truck smacked into me too."

Frowning slightly, Wendy asked, "What's the matter with you?"

Emily shook her head. "Oh, I got something wrong inside. Been kinda ailing since the day I was born. Doctors just shake their heads. I mean, I'm not gonna drop over dead anytime soon, at least I hope not. But I can't run around and stuff. Just gotta walk slowly."

"Do you have cancer or something like that?"

Chuckling, Emily said, "Strange as it may seem, I'd be better off if I did. They can do a lot of stuff with cancer nowadays. No, picked up something new recently that nobody is supposed to have anymore."

Wendy watched Feathers gobble down a chunk of bread. "So, what is it?"

The other girl stumbled slowly to her feet, her eyes not leaving the duck. "Ever heard of TB?"

Wendy gasped. "Tuberculosis? You have tuberculosis?"

"Bingo."

"I thought they—"

"Yeah," Emily interrupted, "everyone thought they'd gotten rid of that nasty little disease years and years ago. 'Cept the TB bacteria changed themselves enough so the vaccinations don't work anymore for some people. I've got a modern version of an old killer. Lucky me."

As if to clear her thoughts, Wendy shook her head. "So, what do you—"

"Listen, I've gotta go do some studying," the girl said, pointing toward the school building. "Here, you and Feathers can finish my lunch for me." She paused and studied the bird resting comfortably in the box. "Hey, Wendy, thanks for taking such good care of him. It's not fun to hurt. It's not fun at all."

With that she ambled away, her walk slow and steady, her feet shuffling slightly as she moved past the kick-ball game that filled the playground with excited laughter. No one paid any attention to her as she passed by. Everyone was too intent on the game, on the runners, on the score.

Wendy sat in silence for a long moment watching a girl lost in a crowd, surrounded by activity and laughter. And all that girl could do was shuffle slowly past without anyone noticing her, without being a part of the world in which she moved.

With a sigh, Wendy tossed the last remnants of her lunch in Feather's direction. The bird sniffed at it, then turned his head.

✧ ✧ ✧

School buses vied for position as long lines of children clamored to board. Shouts echoed across the parking lot while diesel fumes tainted the air and crossing guards waved traffic along the roads and driveways fronting the building.

Wendy stood at the far end of the sidewalk, getting madder and madder at Joey Dugan, who hadn't made his appearance yet. Occasionally a group of girls would stroll by, glance at the duck hiding in the box at her feet, giggle to themselves, then hurry away, whispering and pointing over their shoulders.

The school day had finally ended—almost. Now all she had to do was make her escape. Except that Joey hadn't kept his promise of picking her up at exactly 3:00. *Typical male,* she thought with a frustrated shake of her head.

Beep. Beep.

A car squeaked to a halt in front of her, and a smiling face peered from the driver's side. "You look kinda lost," a voice called above the din of departing buses and chatter of students.

Wendy blinked. "Why does Joey Dugan look so much like Ruth Cadena today?" she asked.

"Because Joey Dugan asked me to pick you up," came the pleasant reply. "He had to stay late to finish an unexpected lab assignment. Hope you don't mind."

Opening the back door, Wendy gently lowered the duck box onto the seat. Then she opened the front door and jumped in. "I wouldn't care if he sent the space shuttle to pick me up. Just get me outta here! Take me back to the ranch where I can count everyone around me on two hands without using my toes."

Ms. Cadena chuckled as she guided the automobile away from the curb. "Bad first day, huh?"

"Ever heard of the Gulf War?"

"Yeah," the woman said.

"It was like that," Wendy stated, "except the only bombs that got dropped on me were dirty looks. Of course showing up for class with a duck in your arms isn't going to win you any bonus points in the popularity contest. Everyone thinks I'm a real freak. One guy called me Noah and asked me where I'd parked the ark."

The woman winced. "Ouch. I see what you mean."

Wendy stared out the window, watching the last remnants of Gallatin Gateway flash by. "Well, not everyone was a pain," she confessed. "There was this one girl. Kinda nice, but sorta strange too." Wendy turned to the driver. "Did you know that it's possible to get TB again?"

Ruth Cadena nodded. "Oh, you met Emily Wells. Yeah. She contracted the disease about a year ago."

"You know about her?"

43

"Sure," the woman chuckled, "it's my job. After all, I am a social worker, remember? *And* western director of Project Youth Revival? *And* enthusiastic supporter of Shadow Creek Ranch for three years?"

"And *very special* friend of my dad for those same three years, right?"

Ms. Cadena nodded shyly. "You noticed, huh?"

Wendy grinned, then grew pensive. "So what's with this Emily person? She seems so sad."

"Well, she doesn't exactly have a lot in her life to make her happy. Her folks are struggling financially. Hospital bills have devastated them, to say nothing of watching their only child suffer from a disease that no one is supposed to get. But they seem to be surviving somehow. She has to get X-rays of her chest every month or so and repeated skin tests. Her case is proving to be tricky because today's TB strains seem to be resistant to traditional treatments and medications. From what the doctor told me, her lungs are very damaged."

"Will she get better?"

"Eventually, yes—to a point. But how fast that happens no one knows. I guess it depends on how strong her body is and how hard it can fight to heal itself. For now, all she can do is make the best of a very dangerous situation."

For a long moment Wendy was silent. "I guess I'm kinda lucky, aren't I?"

"We all are."

The car sped along State Highway 191, heading

south toward the towering mountains that rose up ahead like a granite curtain. Wendy watched the bare fields and tree-lined roads flash by. That morning she'd rescued an injured duck who couldn't fly. Now she was wondering what she could do to help a sixth grader who couldn't run.

Seven-year-old Samantha jumped from her perch on the porch and ran to greet Ms. Cadena's car as it rumbled down the long driveway leading to the Station. The girl's face shone with the excitement reserved only for greeting family members whom she hadn't seen for at least five minutes. "I got an A on my spelling test," she called through the open window while holding up a piece of paper with the grade written in bold red ink near the top. "I even spelled 'hotel.' Can you spell 'hotel,' Wendy?"

Wendy grinned broadly as the car moved slowly toward the parking spot under a tall cottonwood. "Hey, that's great, Sam. Good for you! No, I don't think I could spell such a hard word."

Samantha glanced in at the back seat. "What's in the box?" she asked, her breath a little labored from all the excitement and running around.

Wendy jumped out as soon as the car stopped. "It's a duck."

"A duck?" the younger girl gasped. "Did you buy it in Bozeman?"

"No, we hit it in the Gallatin National Forest. Joey's truck and our little friend here were trying to occupy the same spot at the same time. The duck lost."

"Is he dead?"

"No. He's alive and hungry. Poor fella's kinda banged up, so he can't walk or fly yet. But he'll get better, I hope."

Retrieving the box from the back seat, Wendy let Samantha peek inside. "Hello, Duck," Samantha said.

"His name is Feathers."

"Oh, hello, Feathers." The little girl grinned. "I like that name."

The three started walking toward the Station steps. "So," Ms. Cadena said, "are you going to help Wendy take care of the newest member of the ranch?"

"Sure," Samantha stated firmly. "I can even teach it how to spell 'hotel.'"

Tyler Hanson appeared at the second-story balcony as the trio entered the large foyer below. "Hey," he called. "Where's Joey?"

"He had to stay late at the university," Ms. Cadena answered, waving up at the man. "So I picked up our schoolgirl and brought her home."

Wendy glanced up at her father. "I know how disappointed you are," she said. "We'll try not to let it happen again."

The man descended the steps and took Ruth in

his arms. "Oh, I think I'll get over it," he said, gazing into her eyes. "Hi, Beautiful," he whispered.

Glancing at Samantha, Wendy said, "Why do I get the impression that we just became invisible?"

The younger girl giggled. "I think they like each other . . . a lot."

Ms. Cadena blushed. "Tyler, aren't you going to say hello to your daughter?"

"Daughter?" the man frowned. "I have a daughter?"

Wendy rolled her eyes. "It's like Debbie and Barry all over again."

Mr. Hanson scooped up the girl with his arms and lifted her off the floor. "Wendy! My sweet Wendy! Oh, yes, I remember you. Likes to ride a horse named Early, gets up before air, and never, ever gets into any kinda trouble no matter how hard she tries." He paused. "When did you get so big?"

Staring at her father nose to nose, Wendy giggled, "Maybe you should put me down before you hurt yourself."

He lowered her back onto the polished wood floorboards. "They grow up too fast," he said, almost to himself. "Much too fast."

"Well," Wendy stated, bending down and picking up her box, "while you contemplate the years as they roll by, I've got to get Feathers something to eat and a comfortable place to sleep here in the Station."

"Feathers? What's a Feathers?" Mr. Hanson asked.

Ms. Cadena smiled and took his arm in hers. "I'll explain everything if you'll join me for a short walk down by Shadow Creek."

Wendy watched the two adults amble out of the Station hand in hand and head for the distant footbridge. She sighed. Romance still puzzled her, but, for some unexplainable reason, it seemed a little less disgusting lately. Maybe her dad was right. Perhaps she was growing up.

A loud *quack, quack* from the box brought her thoughts back to the present. Love could wait. Now she had a hungry duck to feed. She and Samantha headed for the kitchen where the clank of pots and pans meant Grandma was beginning to fix supper. Sometimes the mysteries of life just had to make way for the reality of hungry waterfowl.

Evening shadows threaded their way among the cottonwoods and pines at the far end of the pasture. The air turned from chilly to cold, sending forest creatures deep into dens and the human inhabitants of Shadow Creek Ranch to their favorite spots before the roaring fire in a den of their own.

Joey yawned broadly and stretched his long legs as Samantha dozed by his knees. Grandpa Hanson turned the pages of a ranching magazine while his wife munched on kernels of popcorn left over from supper.

Wendy busied herself with newly assigned homework, allowing the warmth of the fireplace to wash over her like billowy waves from a hot sea. She glanced up to see Mr. Hanson and Ms. Cadena enter the den both laughing over some shared secret. They found a spot together on the long couch by the bookcase and settled in for an evening of relaxation. The lawyer surveyed the high-ceilinged room with satisfaction. "Isn't this great?" he said. "Just like a Grandma Moses painting, although she usually didn't include a duck in her images."

Feathers, who was resting among the folds of a fluffy towel in his box, looked up as if to say, "Well, maybe Grandma Moses didn't recognize the true potential of including mallards in her masterpieces."

Ms. Cadena sighed. "I miss Debbie and Barry. I hope they're having a good time in Mexico while our favorite wrangler checks out those horses. He's got a good eye for livestock, that's for sure. Any animals he selects will make a wonderful addition to the Shadow Creek herd."

Grandpa Hanson grinned. "I told them to think of the trip as an extended honeymoon. Debbie thought that perhaps looking at horses all day long might not be the most romantic activity for newlyweds, but, hey, they're in Mexico, and I'm paying all expenses. She promised she'd do her best to keep Wrangler Barry from getting lost in his work."

Wendy tapped her pencil on her paper. "How do you spell 'Argentina'?"

Samantha's eyes popped open. "H-o-t-e-l," she said.

"That's *hotel,*" the girl by the fireplace chuckled.

"Yeah, I know," Samantha said proudly. "If you ever need to know how to spell it, just ask me."

"I think it's A-r-g-e-n-t-i-n-a," Grandma Hanson called.

"Thanks," Wendy said. "I'm supposed to write a report on it and figured I probably should spell it correctly." She was silent for a moment. "Do you think people get tuberculosis in Argentina?"

Mr. Hanson blinked. "What?"

"Tuberculosis. You know, TB. There's this girl at school named Emily who has it. She looks pretty bad. I wish I could help her."

Ms. Cadena leaned forward. "You can," she said softly.

Wendy glanced over at her. "How?"

"By being her friend. By not laughing at her. By understanding her limitations."

The girl thought for a minute. "I may as well. After today my classmates aren't exactly standing in line to get to know me. They all think I'm from Mars. Guess I don't blame 'em."

The woman held Wendy's gaze with hers. "You told me that one person doesn't think you're from Mars. She even shared her lunch with the very focus of everyone's laughter. You see, Wendy, you don't have to earn someone's friendship by being a certain way or acting like everyone else.

50

Friendship comes through acceptance, and I think someone accepted you today, duck and all."

The girl nodded slowly, then sighed. "I'm getting confused by all this. I'm in a strange school with strange people. I don't know *how* to act or what to think anymore."

Ruth Cadena rose and walked across the room to settle beside Wendy. "I don't blame you," she said. "But that doesn't change the fact that a young girl needs you to be her friend. This ranch exists to help people, young people with problems. You're part of this ranch. That means that even in strange schools with strangers, you have a work to do, a promise to keep. So why don't you think of Emily as a guest here on Shadow Creek, as someone with a real problem. No, her parents haven't deserted her. Nor is she in any trouble with the law, but she's still hurting inside. She needs what you've learned to give while living on this ranch." The woman paused. "What do you say, Wendy? Will you take on the responsibility of helping her?"

Wendy's eyes narrowed slightly. "You knew about Emily all along, didn't you? When you found out that Lizzy was going back to New York for a while, you told Dad to send me to Lewis and Clark, didn't you?"

Ms. Cadena smiled. "Hey, it's my job, remember?"

The girl shook her head, a cautious grin lifting the corners of her mouth. "How did you know we'd meet, that she'd talk to me?"

"Because I know Emily and she's a great kid." Glancing at the box by the fireplace, the woman added, "Sometimes birds of a feather like to gather together. You needed a friend. She needed a friend. Mission accomplished."

The girl frowned. "Mission *not* accomplished. She was friendly all right, sorta. But she still stayed off by herself most of the day. Besides, she was more interested in the duck than me."

"Maybe she identified with the bird. Both she and it are hurting, both are stuck dealing with a lot of pain. And both feel out of place, as if they don't fit in."

"Yeah," Wendy agreed. "That makes sense, I guess. But I can't take the duck with me every day just so she can have someone to be miserable with."

Ms. Cadena stared at her for a long moment. "Why not?"

Wendy's eyes widened. "Wait a minute. Wait just a big, huge Montana minute, here. You're not saying that I should take Feathers to school with me again? It was a disaster! Everybody laughed at me and made quacking sounds behind my back. You can't be serious!"

Ms. Cadena smiled gently. "You're the first person Emily has talked to since the school year began. She probably feels comfortable with you because of how you treat that injured animal. And she feels safe in your presence because she knows you know how to care for something *or someone* in pain."

Wendy closed her eyes and let out a long moan. "Man oh man. Helping people can sure be embarrassing sometimes."

Ruth nodded. "So what do you say, Wendy Hanson? Wanna give it a try? After all, you live on Shadow Creek Ranch. Being helpful is in the water out here. You can't stop yourself."

Peering into the box, Wendy studied the now sleeping mallard, his head tucked securely under one somewhat disheveled wing. "Miss Elrod will have a cat."

"You leave Esther Elrod to me," the woman said softly.

Wendy sighed, then nodded. "Oh, OK. I guess I don't have anything to lose except my sanity and every hope I ever had for a normal dating life."

Mr. Hanson's head jerked up from his reading. "Dating life?" he gasped. "Did you say *dating* life?"

His daughter grinned. "Did I?"

Ms. Cadena reached over and hugged her young friend. "You won't be sorry," she said. "Really, Wendy, you won't be sorry."

Outside, the cold winds of late autumn moaned among the bare branches of the trees surrounding the Station. Inside, snuggled safely in the den, the inhabitants of Shadow Creek Ranch rested from their busy day. But one of those feeling the warmth of the fire couldn't relax completely. Because of her belief in what the ranch stood for, she was going to return to her new school and try her best to touch the life of someone who was hurting. Wendy stared at the flickering fire for a long time, then returned to her studies, an uncomfortable fear growing deep inside her. Would she be strong enough to accomplish her goal? After all, she was just a human being. And as unbelievable as it may seem, she just might be forced to spend sixth grade in the company of a duck.

CHAPTER 3

The Bully

Since waving goodbye to Grandpa Hanson and climbing aboard the big yellow school bus where the road to Shadow Creek Ranch met Highway 191, Wendy had sat silently contemplating her fate. All around her were the whispers, giggles, and barnyard sounds she'd come to expect.

Her first challenge that morning had been to convince the bus driver that the box held tightly in her arms contained a school project, which it did— kinda. But it was the thought of facing the strange woman she'd met the day before when she first entered the school building that got Wendy really nervous. Somehow she and Ms. Cadena would have to persuade the registrar that Feathers needed to attend classes as much as she did.

When she arrived at the school she found the hallways crowded with noisy young people. Wendy made her way to the office, still clinging to the cardboard container with its injured occupant.

Closing the door behind her, she stood waiting to face the challenge.

"May I help you?" a hurried voice called from behind the file cabinets across the room.

"Yes, ma'am," Wendy responded. "I need to make arrangements for another . . . ah . . . classmate . . . sorta."

"Certainly," came the quick reply as the woman crossed the room and seated herself before the archaic piece of office equipment. As before, the registrar never looked in Wendy's direction, so intent was she on her work. She adjusted her glasses, then poised her fingers above the keys. "Name?" she asked.

"Feathers," Wendy responded with a nod.

The woman typed quickly. "Last name?"

Wendy blinked. "Ah . . . Mallard?"

"Mallard," the woman repeated as she pounded the word onto the paper. "Sounds foreign. Grade?"

Wendy thought for a moment. "First. Yeah, definitely first."

"That would make him . . . it is a him, isn't it?"

"Yes."

"That would make him about 6 years old, right?"

The girl shrugged. "Sounds good to me."

"OK," the typist announced, ripping the paper out of the typewriter and holding it at arm's length while fishing in her desk drawer with her free hand. "Just take this form to the child's guardian, have him or her fill in all but the shaded

56

portions, and sign at the bottom. Place the completed form in this envelope, seal it, and return it to me. Is the student here today?"

Glancing at the box, Wendy answered, "Yes, ma'am."

For the first time, the registrar looked in Wendy's direction. "Then have him go directly to Mrs. Emerald's room—that's 1-A—and tell her the enrollment process has begun. Has Feathers attended kindergarten?"

"Probably not."

"Then I won't be needing to update previous records." The woman nodded, then hurried back to her filing cabinets to continue searching for whatever was hiding behind them. "Make sure all blanks are filled in and tell young Mr. Mallard welcome to Lewis and Clark. Will that be all?"

"Yes, ma'am."

"By the way," the registrar called, "have you seen a set of keys? There's five on a ring with a little tag that says, 'Have a nice day.'"

"No, ma'am. I haven't seen them."

She heard the registrar sigh. "Have a nice day," the woman called.

With a nod Wendy left the room, carrying the box in front of her.

As she was beginning to make her way to her locker, weaving through running classmates, she heard a familiar male chuckle. "Well, if it isn't Noah and her duck. Do I say hello or just quack?"

Ignoring the speaker, she kept walking along the crowded hallway.

"What's the matter, duck got your tongue?"

The girl tightened her grip on the box. Dad had told her that, in a new school, she'd find some individuals who seemed to take pleasure in teasing people. One of those freaks of nature just had latched onto her.

"Tell you what," the boy called, "I'll trade you three chickens and a pig for that critter. I'm getting kinda hungry for duck soup."

"Leave her alone!" Wendy heard someone respond in a raspy tone. She frowned. Where had she heard that voice before?

"Well, well, if it isn't Breathless in Montana."

"Just leave her alone," the unseen girl repeated. "She's doing a good thing, taking care of that duck." The words sounded labored and strained.

"Mind your own business," the boy warned.

Wendy slowed slightly.

"You woulda probably just left that duck by the side of the road, wouldn't you?" the other girl stated. "You woulda let it die there or get eaten by some wild animal. That's what you woulda done."

"Back off!" the boy shouted, anger driving his words. "What's it to you, anyway? You're no better than that stupid duck."

Suddenly silence filled the hallway. Only the girl's raspy breathing and the distant roar of departing school buses broke the stillness. Without saying a word, Wendy placed the box gently on the floor, turned, and walked through the motionless crowd to where the boy was standing. He was just a little taller than she, slightly overweight with short curly hair and thin slits for eyes. Emily Wells stood off to one side, face buried in her hands, her sobs choked and labored.

Wendy stuck her nose within an inch of the boy's. "My name is Wendy, not Noah. And, no, I don't want to trade my duck. Also, I'd appreciate it if you'd be a little nicer to my friend Emily. Do we understand each other?"

The boy stood his ground. "Why don't you go back to your ranch and stay there with all the other animals?"

"I will," Wendy said, "this afternoon. Until then, I've got to go to class. So do you. If you stay out of my way, and I stay out of your way, everything will be fine."

"What's with you?" he sneered. "I was just teasing."

Nodding, Wendy said, "Making fun of me is OK. Making fun of my duck is fine, too. We don't mind. We can take it. But you were just mean to someone who can't defend herself. And that makes me angry."

The boy chuckled, still standing nose to nose with her. "You don't scare me," he said.

Wendy smiled. "I should."

The class bell clanged loudly, piercing the heavy tension like a sharp knife. Young people scurried away, glancing over their shoulders at the two sixth graders facing each other. Finally, Wendy turned and walked to where she'd placed the box. Picking it up, she glanced around. The hallway was emptying fast. Emily had disappeared.

The morning passed as if in slow motion. Each tick of the large clock above the blackboard seemed to last an hour. Wendy tried to concentrate on what Miss Elrod was saying, but she kept glancing at the empty seat near the back, the spot Emily had occupied the day before. What had happened to her? Where had she gone after the confrontation in the hallway?

Nearby sat the boy whose name Wendy learned was Garwin Huffinger, a title the girl decided would turn any normal person into a jerk. He would stare at her from time to time, his expression as if bullets were shooting from his eyes and cutting her down where she sat.

Finally, noon arrived and with it an opportunity to search for the missing girl. The first place Wendy explored was the logical choice—the infirmary at the far end of the main hall.

"Yes, Emily Wells was here earlier today," the pretty young nurse behind the desk said, placing her half-eaten sandwich on a napkin and taking a tiny swig of milk from the pint container next to her apple. "Poor girl. She has these attacks. Can't breathe. Her doctor has me put her on pure oxygen for a few minutes. Seems to help." The woman pointed at a tall metal cylinder propped against a corner of the room. A thin, blue, plastic mask dangled from it by lengths of clear tubing. "She rested for a while here on the examining table, then seemed to be all right." The woman shook her head. "What a way to live. Poor girl."

After eying the device for a long moment, Wendy turned to the nurse. "Do you know where she is now?"

"In class, I guess."

Wendy shook her head. "I didn't see her all morning. Maybe she went home or something."

The nurse frowned. "No, I would've had to sign her out if that was the case." She brightened. "Emily has to be somewhere on the school grounds. Why not check the ball field or bus parking area? If you don't find her, stop by again and I'll get security on her trail. She'll show up. It's a big school, but not that big."

With a nod, Wendy said, "OK. Thanks."

As she walked down the hallway, she paused at Miss Elrod's homeroom door to check on Feathers. There, kneeling by the box, surrounded by the emptiness of an abandoned classroom, sat Emily talking quietly to the mallard, stroking its feathers while resting her head on the bookcase next to her.

Wendy entered silently and stood by the

blackboard, watching. *What must it be like to have to fight for breath sometimes? What must it be like to know that certain parts of your body, important parts like the lungs, have been damaged and can't function fully like normal people's? How do you live with that? How is it possible to survive not being able to stand up for yourself because it takes too much energy, too much breath?*

"I missed you this morning," Wendy said softly. "I kept watching for you, but you never came to class."

The other girl didn't look up. She just kept stroking the sleeping bird. "I . . . I had to do something."

"Yeah, I know. I just talked to the nurse."

The girl frowned. "Now you know all my deep dark secrets. You can laugh if you want to."

"I'd never laugh about something like that," Wendy said firmly. "Your notebook, the one with the sunglasses on it? That I'd laugh about. Or maybe your desk. What's with all those drawings of flowers on the front? Now, *that's* funny."

The soft wrinkles of a grin creased Emily's pale face. "So I'm no artist."

"Artist? My horse can draw better flowers."

The grin broadened. "Don't make me laugh too much, Wendy. Takes a lot of air to laugh."

Wendy felt a lump rise in her throat. Emily didn't even have enough breath to laugh? "Sorry.

62

I'll keep my jokes on the tee-hee, not the ha-ha level. Deal?"

"Deal," Emily said with a smile, then paused. "How's Feathers doin' today?"

Walking across the room, Wendy sat down at her desk. "He's OK. Ate more breakfast than I did. But I think he's hungry again."

Emily glanced up at her. "Well, go get him some lettuce or something. He's already gobbled down most of my lunch."

Wendy nodded. "OK. You keep him company and I'll see what the cafeteria has that might interest a hungry waterfowl. Maybe they've got a fresh shipment of grubs and spiders. I understand that ducks love grubs and spiders. Would you like some too?"

Slowly Emily lifted her hand. "Take it easy. That's pretty close to a ha-ha joke if you ask me."

"Sorry. I'll just get some boring lettuce and bread. Totally unfunny food. Might even make you cry if you let 'em. Would that be better?"

Emily shook her head. "You're *crazy,* Wendy."

"I've heard that comment from people who are supposed to love me," the girl called over her shoulder. "So you're in good company. I'll be right back, OK?"

"Me and Feathers will be waiting for you," came the gentle reply.

After stopping by the infirmary to let the nurse know that she had found the missing student, Wendy hurried to the cafeteria and gathered what she and her duck might like to eat. Then she returned.

While the bird enjoyed crisp leaves of lettuce and milk-soaked pieces of bread, Wendy attacked her vegetable plate and side of rice. Both girl and bird seemed pleased with her choices.

"Tell me about your ranch," Emily invited after a few minutes. "Is it pretty?"

"Sure," Wendy answered between chews. "It's like a lot of other mountain ranches in Montana, only more beautiful. At least I think so."

"Does it have lots of trees and flowers on it?"

Wendy paused. "Yeah. And a stream that runs right by the house and lots of pastures and meadows and stuff. It's your normal amazing, wonderful, ranch."

Emily hesitated. "And birds? Does it have lots of birds there too?"

For a long moment Wendy studied her new friend. "You've never been on a horse ranch, have you?"

"No."

"You've never been outside of Bozeman, either. Right?" A shake of the head. "Why?"

Holding a lettuce leaf for Feathers to examine, Emily said, "My folks, they kinda don't have a car anymore. When we did, my dad only had enough gas in it to go to work and back. Now, when we want to go shopping, we take the bus or a neighbor lets us ride to the store with him. I've seen the mountains in the distance. They look so peaceful, so beautiful. And I've seen the big birds sailing high in the sky, going around and around, just floating without even flapping their wings. I know they must live in the mountains 'cause I've never seen any of them land in the city. Flying looks like fun. You can go anywhere you want and just ride the air. It'd be nice to be a bird, don't you think, Wendy?"

Wendy felt a lump lodge in her throat. "Yeah. It would."

"And here's poor Feathers. He can't even fly, so he has to eat lettuce from the fingers of people he doesn't even know. But he's doing OK, see? He's not scared or anything. Although he can't fly, he's doing OK, right Wendy?"

The other girl nodded. "Listen, Emily, I've got an idea, but I can't talk to you about it right now. I've gotta check with my grandpa and stuff. But until I do, will you promise me something?"

"Sure."

"I don't want you to stick up for me like you did this morning. Creeps like Garwin can be trouble. I mean *big* trouble. Just keep out of his way. Do you promise?"

Emily glanced at her. "I didn't like what he was saying to you."

"I know," Wendy smiled at her, "and I really, *really* appreciate what you did. But I've met a lot of people like Garwin. He's just a hot air balloon, all puffed up and full of gas." Her friend grinned at her description. "So let me deal with him, OK? He can't hurt me. But he can hurt you. My dad calls me a bulldozer, and I guess sometimes I act like one." Wendy pointed at Garwin's unoccupied desk. "It's just not fair when someone like him dumps on someone like you."

"Because I'm sick?" the other girl asked coldly, her smile fading.

"No," Wendy said softly, "because you're Emily Wells who isn't *anything* like a bulldozer."

The girl frowned. "Are you saying you want to be my bodyguard or something?"

"No, I just want to be your friend."

Emily sat for a moment, contemplating what Wendy had just said. All of it was new to her. Never in her young life had someone come out and said they wanted to be her friend. Even before she had contracted tuberculosis, she'd been a sickly child, shy and reserved, the one who sat by herself in a crowded room, the student who never raised her hand in class.

"Why?" she asked. "Why do you want to be my friend?"

Wendy studied the thin, gaunt lines etched across her companion's face. "Well, I'm a girl with a duck. And you're the first student who talked to me without making an animal sound or saying I was weird. I figure it's you or no one."

Chuckling, Emily let her expression relax into

a grin. "OK. Fair enough. We can be friends."

"Great. Now, since we're officially long-lost buddies, I need for you to help me take care of ol' Feathers here and also come to my rescue on the South America assignment. I've never set foot in the place, yet I hate it with all my heart."

Emily laughed. "I like South America! It's got mountains and rivers and jungles and parrots. Who doesn't love a parrot?"

"I think I'll just concentrate on this particular bird for a while," Wendy said, frowning and motioning toward the box, "although, I must say, if Joey was driving in South America he'd probably run into a parrot too. He seems to be very good at hitting flying wildlife with his truck."

With the sounds of recess drifting through the tall glass windows, the two girls settled in beside the box and opened their textbooks to read the next day's geography assignment. For now, short-haired bullies and long metal oxygen tanks would have to wait.

Traffic was particularly heavy as Grandpa Hanson guided the ranch pickup truck through the maze of back streets and headed for the farm co-op at the east end of Bozeman. Wendy sat on the passenger side of the cab, watching the houses and garages slip by, feeling relaxed and happy. It was Friday afternoon, and Friday afternoons meant three things. First, school was closed for the next two days. Even if she showed up at the front door of Lewis and Clark there'd be no one to let her in, a thought she found thoroughly refreshing. Second, she and Grandpa Hanson were paying their weekly visit to the feed and supply store, an activity she savored with the same intensity that one girl she happened to know experienced when visiting the fashion apparel departments of upscale Manhattan retailers.

Last, but certainly not least, was the fact that on Fridays Grandpa always took her to Charlie's, an ice-cream shop located across the street from the Baxter Hotel. No school, musty-smelling sacks of high-grade oats, and a big dish of Rocky Road—what more could life possibly offer?

"Grandpa?"

"Yes?"

The girl thought for a minute. "Is it OK for us to be happy when someone we know is sad?"

Grandpa Hanson nodded slowly. "I don't see why not."

"Why?"

"Because God wants us to be happy, even in a sad world. Happiness, I mean real happiness, the kind that comes from pure love, close family relations, and being one with nature, is supposed to remind us of heaven to come. It's sorta like a sneak preview of eternity with Jesus. I believe that's a good reason to be joyful."

Wendy frowned slightly. "I've been feeling kinda guilty whenever I laughed because of someone at school who can't."

"Can't laugh?"

"Yeah. Isn't that sad? If she laughs too hard, she can't breathe because her lungs are bad."

"Oh, you mean Emily?"

"Yeah. I can't even tell her my funniest stories because I don't want to make her have to put on an oxygen mask and lie still on a table in the infirmary. So I just tell her my sorta funny stories."

Grandpa Hanson smiled to himself. "That is a problem, isn't it?"

Wendy glanced at her grandfather then back out at the street. "I was wondering something."

"What?"

"Well, Emily has never been out of Bozeman. Her folks are really poor, and they don't go anywhere. Now, don't get me wrong. I think Bozeman is a great place, a *whole* lot nicer than New York City. I mean, the air here doesn't smell like a truck barfed in your face, the people actually look at you when you pass them on the sidewalk, and the biggest traffic jam we've ever been in is when the high school had a parade and we had to go two whole blocks out of our way. Oh, and the taxi drivers speak English. How wonderful is *that?*"

"Astonishing!"

"Anyway, like I was saying, Emily has never

been out of Bozeman, and I know that with Lizzy gone we're kinda shorthanded out on the ranch, but if you think it would be all right, I mean, I could help do stuff like clean clothes and sweep floors and—"

Her grandfather lifted his hand. "We'd be happy for Emily to come out to Shadow Creek for a visit."

The girl blinked. "You would? I mean, can she?"

The old man smiled. "It's not like we've never had young people on the property before."

Wendy chuckled. "Yeah, but that was different. You know, planned and stuff, and Lizzy was helping Grandma and Barry was doing the horse thing and Debbie was doing the nature thing. Now Debbie and Barry are in Mexico, and Lizzy's out on Long Island. Everybody's so busy with schoolwork and chores and stuff—"

"Sweetheart," Grandpa Hanson interrupted again, "it's OK. She's welcome anytime as long as her parents say she can come. And if you're planning for her to stay more than a few days, you'll need to check with Ruth Cadena and Emily's doctor."

"Great! Stop," the girl said.

"Stop?"

"Yeah stop, right here."

The old man steered the vehicle to the curb and set the emergency brake. "What's going on?"

Wendy grinned. "See that house over there,

the one with the little porch and swing set in the front yard?"

"Yes."

"That's Emily's house. I asked her where she lived, and she told me all about her street. I thought it sounded familiar. Then I remembered how you always go to the feed store on this back road, and that's when I figured out where she lived. Right there. We've been passing her house every Friday and I didn't even know it. Amazing, huh?"

Grandpa Hanson chuckled. "And you thought that, as long as we were in the neighborhood, we could stop by and invite her out to Shadow Creek Ranch for the weekend?"

The girl shrugged. "If it was OK with you."

The old man shook his head. "Why do I get the impression that you're in charge of the world and I just work for you?"

"Because," the girl stated while opening the door and slipping out into the cold air, "you want everyone to be happy, same as me."

The rancher watched his granddaughter run along the cracked sidewalk and climb the unpainted steps of the old house on the corner. A rusting car rested on cement blocks in the front yard and an old, abandoned doghouse guarded the pathway leading to the backyard. He heard Wendy knock on the door.

Looking up from her book, Emily saw the outline of someone standing on the porch. Slowly, methodically, she got out of her chair and walked to the door. "Who is it?" she called as loudly as she could.

"The capital of Argentina is Buenos Aires, and its chief export is raw meat, which doesn't do me one bit of good, 'cause I don't touch the stuff."

"I'm coming, I'm coming!" Emily grinned broadly to herself.

Placing a heavy coat over her shoulders and grabbing a small suitcase huddled next to the door, she hurried out into the sunlight. "Is it really OK? Am I really going to your ranch?"

Eyeing the suitcase, Wendy blinked. "Yeah, ah, Grandpa said you're welcome anytime, which is what I knew he'd say. That's why I invited you even before I asked him. I couldn't wait!" She hesitated. "But first we've gotta ask your mom and dad."

"They said it's OK."

"They did?"

"Yup. Then, let's *go!*"

Wendy glanced at the suitcase, then the girl. "Well . . . great. Yeah. Let's go." In a slight state of confusion, she took the satchel from the girl's slender hand and guided her friend down the steps. Arm in arm they strolled at an even, nonhurried pace out to the curb where an old farm truck waited, engine rumbling expectantly. "I take it you're Emily," Grandpa Hanson called, stepping down from the cab and extending his hand. "I'm—"

"You're Grandpa Hanson; I know," Emily breathed, barely able to contain her excitement.

"Wendy has told me all about you. She says you're the best grandfather in all the world and can snore louder than a bull moose in rut."

The old man grinned. "Yup. That's me."

He helped the new passenger up into the cab and fastened her seat belt for her. Then he and Wendy hopped in too and, in a few seconds, they headed down the street once again. "My parents said to tell you thank you for letting me visit your ranch," Emily said politely, smiling up at the driver. "They even got me a bird book from the library, see?" She held up a worn copy of *Field Guide to Western Birds* by Roger Tory Peterson.

Wendy raised her hand. "Wait a minute. When did your folks get you that book?"

"Last Wednesday."

"How did they know you were coming out to Shadow Creek Ranch?"

Emily thought for a minute. "Ms. Cadena came over and talked with them Tuesday night."

"And . . . when did I show up at Lewis and Clark for the first time?"

"Monday."

Closing her eyes, Wendy sighed. "So Ms. Cadena and your folks knew that I was going to ask you to come out to the ranch even before I talked to you about it yesterday?"

Emily nodded. "I didn't want to get my hopes up until you'd actually asked me yourself, which I really, really hoped you would. And you did."

Wendy leaned forward. "And you?" she said, staring at her grandfather. "You were in on this too?"

The man nodded. "Looks like we all know our Wendy pretty well, huh?"

His granddaughter shook her head. "Everyone had figured out what I was going to do even before *I* figured out what I was going to do!" She glanced again at the driver. "Who works for whom?"

Grandpa Hanson grinned broadly. "We all answer to the same Boss," he said with a wink, pointing skyward.

The truck rumbled down the street, leaving swirling leaves in its wake. Emily didn't care who knew what and when and why. All that mattered to her was that she was going to visit the mountains where nature's most wonderful secrets hid among the shadows, and where birds soared high overhead, dancing with the wind and the clouds.

Opening her eyes, Emily stared into the dim, gray light filling the room. Unfamiliar patterns appeared on the wallpaper. A strange wooden lamp rested on a nearby table. Across the small chamber a bookcase marshaled rows of books, some volume boasting bindings bright with color, others dressed in faded leather jackets or worn paper covers.

Where was she? And what were those mysterious sounds filtering through the window?

Slowly she rose on one elbow and waited for her brain to catch up to her senses. This wasn't her bedroom in Bozeman. Nor was this her wallpaper, her bookcase, or her lamp.

Then she remembered, and with the realization came a smile. No, she wasn't home in her bed. She was deep in the mountains, nestled in the arms of Shadow Creek Ranch with Wendy and her dad, Joey and Grandpa and Grandma Hanson and Samantha and Pueblo the dog.

Emily settled back against her pillow, a satisfied sigh escaping her aching chest. Yes, she was at Shadow Creek Ranch. Even the name sounded mysterious and wonderful. Yesterday afternoon, Wendy had snatched her out of Bozeman, away from the traffic and noise, the hustle and bustle of the town, and brought her to a place that had lived only in her imagination.

She'd watched the mountains move majestically toward them as they'd traveled south on the highway. Then the cliffs and towering trees had enveloped them, completely surrounding the truck as it sped along. In a matter of minutes they'd passed from a flat valley to a magical world filled with sparkling streams, granite outcroppings, and pine forests nestled against a hundred hillsides.

And the smell! She'd marveled at the fragrance. No traffic fumes. No lawn fertilizers. No hot, soapy odors spilling from the corner

Laundromat or greasy scents drifting from fast-food restaurants.

No roadside billboards begged for attention. No glaring storefronts or mercury-vapor-flooded parking lots blinded her vision. All of that was gone, replaced by an amazing, body-tingling sensation of freedom, of purity, of absolute nothingness but the presence of nature. The girl had reveled in it, drinking in its energy like a thirsty traveler lost in a desert, allowing the feelings and scents and sounds to swirl about her.

Then had come the evening. No previous experiences in her life could compare with the hours she had spent there between sundown and slumber. There'd been singing, storytelling, gentle laughter, and best of all—silence. Silence in a gathering of people with only the crackling of the logs in the fireplace and the distant whisper of the wind to mark the passing of time. Who would have ever thought that silence could be so beautiful? For minutes on end, no one had spoken. No one had needed to turn on a radio or television to bring entertainment into the cozy den as stars drifted in the night sky. The delicious silence was enough, allowing into each mind the music of creative thought, the conversation of imagination, and the peace of knowing that the week had passed with each having done their best.

Now, as the dawning day appeared in the eastern sky, Emily still couldn't believe that it was real, that she was here in the mountains, among people who treated her with respect and gentle understanding.

Sure, her parents loved her, but she knew her condition worried them. They hurt when she hurt, cried when she cried, and held her during the bad times when her chest ached so much she couldn't sleep or even move. She felt guilty for all the nights she'd kept them awake, for all the money they'd spent for doctor visits and medicines, for the lost hours of work and sleep.

Now, she was in the mountains and they were back in Bozeman. Her parents could sleep all night—and all day—if they wanted to. They could spend time together instead of worrying about her. For a few days they could live life the way it used to be, before the disease struck, before it took her breath away.

A gentle knock sounded at her door. Emily's eyebrows rose. Who'd be calling on her so early in the morning? "Come in?" she said softly.

Wendy's smiling face emerged from the shadows. "You awake?"

"Yeah. Been awake for a few minutes."

The Hanson girl entered quietly and closed the door behind her. "You too, huh? I always get up early—I mean *really* early—except when there's something I don't want to do, then I can sleep 'til noon. But that's not very often. I usually want to get up 'cause there's always something interesting to do around here."

Emily nodded and watched her friend settle in beside her. "I like your ranch," she said.

"Yeah. It's kinda nice, huh?"

The two lay without speaking for a few minutes. "So," Emily said, "what're we doin' today?"

Her companion yawned. "Well, for starters, we're going to church. Then—"

"Church? Really? I haven't been to services for a long time."

"How come?"

Emily sighed. "Well, my dad says that any God who lets a kid like me get TB doesn't deserve to be worshiped. Did God make me get sick? Is that why it happened?"

Wendy frowned. "Nah. God doesn't do stuff like that. Germs and viruses make people sick, and He hates it as much as we do. That's why He's gonna make a new earth that doesn't have any TB or broken bones or hurt birds."

"Well," Emily stated, adjusting her position on the pillow, "I wish He'd hurry up and get with it."

"Yeah," Wendy agreed, "me too."

After another long pause, Emily asked, "How's Feathers?"

Wendy sat up, a smile lighting her face. "He's better. I was just down in the den, and he almost jumped out of his box. I think it's the lettuce. Lettuce must be good medicine—if you're a duck."

Emily nodded. "Maybe I should try eating lettuce and bugs and spiders for a few days. Maybe it would help me, too."

Wendy sighed. "I think you're already on that diet," she stated. "Both of us are. After all, we eat lunch at Lewis and Clark every day, right?"

The other girl grinned. "You have a point."

"Oh," Wendy said, suddenly jumping out of bed, "I almost forgot. After we get back from church and after we eat lunch, Joey and I are going to help you do something really, really awesome, something I bet you've never done before!"

"Yeah? What?"

Lifting her arms, Wendy said, "This afternoon, Emily Wells, we're going to show you how to fly!"

CHAPTER 4

Planet of Joy

Pastor Webley delivered warm smiles and friendly handshakes to each member of his congregation as they exited the church. In the background, the rich, shrill tones of a small pump organ filled the sanctuary and drifted out through the open door, reverberating across the small parking lot where neat rows of pickup trucks and passenger cars waited. Children called excitedly to each other and laughed as their parents chatted with neighbors and introduced themselves to visitors.

Emily stood off to one side, watching the parade of ranchers and country people pass by, reveling in the sensation of being at a place where happiness seemed to be the unspoken order of the day. Since she'd arrived at the little church by the highway, every song, every speech, every greeting had centered on one central theme, a man named Jesus Christ. For some reason, it seemed to have created an atmosphere of tranquillity among the gathered Montanans.

She'd watched preachers on television shout out their sermons, saying "hallelujah" and "praise the Lord" with almost every breath. Some had even uttered words she didn't understand, rolling their eyes heavenward, mumbling like babies from a foreign land.

But this church service hadn't been like that. Sure, the pastor had spoken excitedly, waving his arms sometimes, lifting his Bible over his head, and moving about like a man on a mission. However, the message was different somehow— simple, easy to understand, with lots of Bible texts and interesting stories. Pastor Webley had spoken about Jesus in words filled with reverence as he told how, when a person follows what the Bible says, our wicked world stops being a place of sadness and becomes transformed into a planet of joy. That had even been the title of his speech.

"Pastor Webley was in good form this morning," Wendy whispered as she joined her friend at the far end of the little lobby. "Thought he was going to jump right out of himself."

Emily nodded. "I liked watching him, and listening to him, too. Is it true?"

"What?"

"All the stuff he said about how we're supposed to think of the world as a planet of joy?"

Wendy shook her head. "Sometimes that's not

easy to do. It even seems impossible. Everybody's got problems, everybody's yelling at everybody else. It's a big fat mess. But then I see a really neat sight like a robin feeding a nest of squawking babies or I hear a coyote howling in the night or I smell the flowers in a springtime meadow or," she paused, "or someone sticks up for me at school when a bully is on my case. That's when I say to myself, 'Wendy, get out of the dumps. Forget the homework and the bullies and the mean stuff people do. It's not *all* bad. Really. There are good things in this world too.' Believe it or not, I get to feelin' better. Of course a big dish of Rocky Road doesn't hurt either."

Emily grinned. "Make that chocolate, and I'm with you."

The two girls ambled over to where Pastor Webley stood, his happy chatter lifting the spirits of everyone around him. "Hello, friend of Wendy," he said, extending his hand toward Emily. "I'm happy you visited our little country church. Please come back again soon."

The girl smiled shyly. "I liked your speech this morning."

The man chuckled. "You should see me when I get *really* excited."

Wendy nodded and winked at Emily. "Like when he talks about heaven. The man goes ballistic."

"Ah, heaven," the pastor said, a look of total rapture lighting his face, "land of endless joys and ceaseless activities. I plan to fly to every corner of the universe just to see what's out there. And after I'm done with that, I'm going to pastor a little chapel on the outskirts of the New Jerusalem and have Jesus Himself as my guest speaker. Yup, when it comes to heaven, I could go on and on."

"And sometimes he does," Wendy giggled.

Emily looked into the warm eyes of the minister. "I want to fly, too, like the birds over the mountains."

Pastor Webley nodded knowingly, then leaned close to his visitor. "On one of my journeys, I'm going to visit the sun."

"The sun?" Emily gasped. "You can't go to the sun. It's too hot."

The minister glanced one way then another as if he was about to reveal a long-guarded secret. "I know," he said. "That's why I'm going at *night*."

After being still for a moment, Emily suppressed a giggle. Wendy rolled her eyes and grabbed her companion's arm. "Let's get out of here. I think Pastor Webley is getting heaven fever again. Next thing you know, he'll have us eating ice cream on Neptune where it's like a million degrees below zero."

The minister smiled broadly and pointed at Wendy. "Now there's an idea. An ice-cream party on an ice-cream planet. Cool!"

The two girls waved and hurried away, laughing at the man's enthusiasm and outlandish ideas.

"I don't know," Emily whispered, "I'm not all that crazy about the sun thing, but that party sounds like fun."

Wendy groaned. "Oh, no. I think you've caught Webley heaven fever too."

Emily paused at the bottom of the church steps and turned to her companion. "Tell me more about it," she said. "Tell me more about heaven."

Her friend thought for a moment. "Imagine Shadow Creek Ranch without weeds, bugs, or Joey Dugan."

"But I like Joey," Emily giggled. "He's funny."

Wendy shook her head sadly and sighed behind a grin. "Girl, you've got a lot to learn."

The two continued out into the parking lot, mingling with the people and enjoying what warmth the late-autumn sun had to offer. Emily glanced up at the mountains towering to the south and east of the little churchyard. High in the deep blue of the sky sailed a hawk, riding the updrafts created by the sloping land, hovering effortlessly over the forests and unseen meadows. She closed her eyes, trying to lock the sight into her memory. *In heaven I will fly,* she said to herself. *In heaven, I will fly higher than the birds.*

At the open door of the church, Pastor Webley stood surveying his congregation. His gaze fell on Emily. He'd heard about the little girl who couldn't run and play like the others, who could only watch the world go by, afraid even to laugh. He, too, glanced toward the bright blue sky and studied the distant form drifting in the void. "Lord Jesus," he prayed softly, "make her wings extra strong. And if You're short a pair, she can have mine."

With that, he stepped back into the church and hurried to join his wife at the organ. She had one more chorus to play, and he didn't want to miss a single note.

✧ ✧ ✧

As she strode into the den, a big smile lighted Wendy's face. "You ready?" she asked.

Emily opened one eye. "I can't move. Grandma Hanson's 'words cannot describe how delicious it is' potpie has taken over my body. I almost finished my whole plate which, for me, is an accomplishment. I feel like the Goodyear blimp, if the Goodyear blimp can be totally happy and totally bloated at the same time."

"I know what you mean," Wendy said with a grin. "I shouldn't have had that second piece of carrot cake, but I'm a weak human being with terrible vices. Potpie and carrot cake just happen to be two of 'em." She paused, and then let out a deep belch just as Mr. Hanson walked into the room.

"Nice job," he said with pride. "We could'a used you in the choir this morning. Some of those base notes in the offertory were *way* beyond reach."

Wendy reddened. "I'm sorry," she breathed, covering her mouth with one hand and her stomach with the other. "I was planning on saving that one for the pasture."

The lawyer glanced at Emily. "I never had a son. However, I have a daughter who can *sound* like a son from time to time. I guess I should be thankful."

Grinning sheepishly, Wendy continued, "I'm really sorry 'bout that, Daddy. It kinda snuck up on me."

"It's all part of the Wendy Hanson mystic," her father said. "That and getting up before Himalayan monks say their morning prayers. I thought you were going riding."

His daughter nodded. "We are, as soon as ol' blimp girl over there gets her body out of that recliner and joins Joey and me at the horse barn."

"Barn? Horse? Riding?" Emily raised her hands in a defensive gesture. "I don't know how to ride a horse."

"This isn't exactly like riding a horse. It's . . . it's more like riding *behind* a horse."

Mr. Hanson chuckled. "Don't worry," he said, smiling over at the young guest. "Whatever Miss Hanson and Mr. Dugan have planed for you, it won't hurt . . . much."

Stumbling out of her chair, Emily peeked through the window into the bright sunlight. "I see Joey. I see horses. But I'm *not* going to ride?"

"Well, yes and no." Wendy shook her head. "Will you come on so I can show you what we have in mind? Trust me. It'll be fun."

A sudden commotion arose in the cardboard box by the fireplace. A feathered head popped up above the lid and dark beady eyes looked around as if to say, "Hey, I wanna have some fun too."

"Not this time, Feathers," Wendy called as she and Emily headed for the arched passageway into the foyer. "You still need more time to heal."

The bird quacked loudly, then settled back onto his soft towel with a sigh. "Humans have all the fun around here," he seemed to say.

Wendy paused. "That reminds me. We've got to finish registering Feathers on Monday and get that form turned in."

"Registering Feathers?" Mr. Hanson asked. "For what?"

"School," his daughter called over her shoulder.

"School?" the man repeated. He watched the two young people leave the den, then settled back into his chair, mumbling softly to himself, "And they say *lawyers* are crazy."

Joey looked up from his work to see Wendy and her young friend crossing the footbridge. "Almost ready," he called as he headed back into the barn. Emily saw him emerge a few seconds later pulling on what looked like a set of long, carved boards. Then a large wagon appeared, sporting four tall, spoked wooden wheels and a seat hovering high over the whole apparatus.

"What's that?" the girl asked.

"This," Joey announced, placing the wagon

tongues on the ground and gesturing with unre-
strained pride, "is a genuine, original buckboard
complete with leather seat, steel-spring platform,
and brass harness attachments. You're lookin' at a
perfectly restored piece of American history
brought back to like-new condition by yours truly
with the help of Samantha and Pueblo the dog."

"What did Samantha do?" Emily asked, admir-
ing the clean lines and smooth, polished surface of
the wagon.

"She watched a lot and spilled wood preserver
on Pueblo the dog."

"Oh."

"Actually, Sam did perform a great service,"
Joey admitted. "Whenever I got really hot and
thirsty, she'd go into the house and get herself a
cool drink."

"Very thoughtful. And Pueblo?"

"Well, he may not've done a whole lot of work
directly on the wagon, but his coat now has a nice
sheen to it."

Emily chuckled softly. "Sounds like you three
were quite a team."

"This buckboard is classy *and* practical," Joey
continued, motioning toward the wagon. "You can
extend the bed for hauling stuff or just ride
around in it for fun. So, how 'bout it? Are you up
for a trip into the mountains?"

The girl beamed. "Oh, yes! I can ride in this
just fine."

"Great," he said, reaching for the long wagon tongue at his feet. "Just stand back and I'll have everything hitched up before you know it."

Glancing over at Wendy, Emily smiled eagerly. "I can't believe this is happening to me. Last week I could only stare at the mountains. Now I'm actually going to ride up into them. I mean, right to the top. Oh, Wendy, thank you. Thank you *so* much!"

Her companion grinned. "Hey. What're friends for? Besides, we have to humor Joey. He did work hard on the wagon, so we should at least agree to take a ride. I just hope this contraption doesn't fall apart under us."

"I heard that," Joey called over his shoulder as he wrestled a set of straps under the wide belly of his powerful horse.

Soon all three sat side by side up on the lofty bench seat. With a whistle and a flip of the reins, the young wrangler guided the horse and wagon over the footbridge and headed down the long driveway leading away from the Station. In a matter of minutes they were deep in the forest, following a road that soon began to climb.

Even before the dust had settled on the driveway, a car turned off the gravel road that ran past the Station and a horn honked its arrival at the ranch. Mr. Hanson glanced out the window and smiled when he saw Ruth Cadena slip from the driver's seat and start for the broad veranda. He met her just as she reached the top step.

"Hey, you," he said with a warm grin. "We missed you at church."

The woman nodded. "I'm sorry, Tyler. But I got a call from the hospital right before I left. One of the kids I'm working with fell off a skateboard and banged up his knee pretty bad. He'll be OK."

"So, why are you looking so sad?"

Ms. Cadena pressed herself into the man's waiting arms. "While I was there, I had a talk with Emily's doctor. The lab results from her last exam are in."

"And?"

"And they don't look good. She's not responding to the most recent medication and treatment. One of her lungs has almost shut down, and the other isn't very far behind."

Mr. Hanson sighed and squeezed her harder. "Oh, Ruth, I'm so sorry."

The two held each other for a long moment, allowing the cold breezes to wash over them as they tried to come to grips with the dismal diagnosis. "You see, she was born with genetically defective lungs, and the TB isn't exactly helping her condition," Ms. Cadena said. "She's growing more and more resistant to drug therapy. They told me there's really nothing else they can do for her here in Bozeman and suggested that her case be transferred to a specialist in Chicago."

The lawyer nodded. "Then that's what you should discuss with her parents."

Ms. Cadena glanced up at the man. "One problem. Her parents have no insurance. None. And they've spent every penny they have trying to beat this thing, but it just keeps getting worse."

"How 'bout a transplant?"

The woman shook her head. "There've been a few lung transplants in conjunction with heart transplants in the past, but they're still too much in the experimental stage." She closed her eyes as tears spilled down her cheeks. "Oh, Tyler, Emily is dying and I can't do a thing about it. I can't give her any medicine, I can't take her someplace to make her well, I can't speak magic words that will cause her lungs to be healthy again. I've just gotta stand by and watch it happen, and it's tearing me up inside. I feel so helpless, so useless."

Mr. Hanson cupped his hands about her chin and lifted her gaze. "Ruth, you are doing something. You're loving her. You're being her friend at a time when she needs friends. And you brought her and Wendy together. Now, I know my youngest has a few problems of her own. She may be rough around the edges, but she knows how to love people. Wendy knows how to give of herself. That's something she's learned since living here on the ranch, something that's been cultivated in her by coming in direct contact with kids like Emily and all the other young people who've stayed with us. So you see, you're really helping two kids at once here. Emily and Wendy need each other, and you made it happen. You did it, Ruth. You."

The woman nodded slowly. "Yeah, but it's not going to make Emily well, is it?"

Mr. Hanson thought for a long moment. "There're two kinds of healing. Sometimes our bodies need help. Other times it's our minds. Seems to me both are important, and both types of healing can change a life for the better."

She gazed into his eyes. "Tyler," she said, "that's what you do for me."

"What?"

"You heal me. You heal my mind when it's sick with worry and grief over one of my children. Did you know that?"

Smiling, the lawyer rested his chin on the dark hair that had fallen over the woman's forehead. He held her tightly, gazing out over the pasture to the mountains beyond. Up there, somewhere, was a girl who was slowly dying and, hopefully, learning to live at the same time.

Joey reined in his horse and brought the buckboard to a bouncing stop. Beside him, Wendy and Emily sat without speaking, staring out at the endless cascade of mountain ranges stretching to the horizon, their summits piercing the low clouds that drifted through the valleys far below.

"Oh my!" Emily breathed, her face radiant with joy. "Look, Wendy, look at that!"

The girl next to her nodded wordlessly. She'd seen this particular vista many times before, but her reaction was always the same. No words could describe what lay before them. Even Tar Boy stood silent as if drinking in the vastness of the scene, letting its grandeur fill every cell of his powerful body.

Finally, Joey sighed. "Ain't no place like this in New York City."

Wendy chuckled. "No place like this anywhere else in the world as far as I'm concerned."

"Look," Emily exclaimed, pointing skyward. "There's a bird up there, a big one. Do you see it?"

The others nodded. "Probably a red-tailed hawk," Wendy stated. "Might even be an eagle."

The three of them watched the creature glide through the cold air, using the air currents to keep him aloft. The bird moved silently through space like a satellite drifting in earth orbit.

Suddenly, Wendy snapped her fingers. "Hey. That reminds me. Joey and I have a surprise for you. Wanna know what it is?"

Emily nodded. "Sure."

"Well, you gotta do something kinda hard, and it might be a little scary."

"What are you talking about?"

For a second Wendy hesitated. "Remember what I told you this morning, about what we were going to do after church and stuff?"

"Yeah. You said something silly about teaching me how to fly."

"So, you wanna try it?"

The other girl frowned. "How can I fly when I can't even run?"

Joey pointed at the horse. "He'll do your running for you."

"But I can't ride horses."

"Don't have to."

Emily shook her head. "What are you guys talking about?"

Slipping from the seat, Wendy stood on the wagon platform. "Get up and climb into the back and we'll show you."

Her frown deepening, Emily said, "You want me to stand in the wagon?"

"Yeah. Just stand right here behind us with your feet on the platform. Spread 'em apart so you won't lose your balance. Then loop your belt through this metal railing that runs across the top of the seat back. See? Like this." Wendy demonstrated with her hands what she had in mind. "That way you're attached to the wagon and won't fall off in case we hit a bump."

Carefully Emily followed the directions, making sure that she securely fastened her belt to the seat back in front of her.

"Now," Wendy cautioned, "you've got to breathe normally. There's no need to huff or puff 'cause you won't be doing any work. It'll just *seem* like you're working, but you're not. You'll just be standing there, OK? Remember to breathe slowly, in and out and in and out no matter what happens."

As she realized what her friends had in mind, Emily began to grin broadly. Ahead of them stretched the relatively smooth surface of a meadow ringed with small windblown bushes and encircled by a grassy road.

Wendy took her place beside Joey and glanced back at her friend. "Are you ready?"

Emily shook her head, trying to keep her breathing steady. "Ready," she whispered.

"Tar Boy," Joey called, his voice bringing the horse to full alertness. "I want you to run like you've never run before." With that he shouted a loud "Heee-yaaa!" and the animal lunged forward, propelling the buckboard and its occupants ahead with neck-bending acceleration. The animal seemed to know the importance of what he was doing, for he put every molecule of energy into his shoulders, flanks, and thundering hooves.

Faster and faster and faster they sped, creating a blur of the dry grass and strewn boulders as they charged across the meadow. Emily felt herself rushing through the air at a dizzying speed. Never in her life had she known such explosive power.

All she could feel was the blast of wind and the incredible sense of freedom that seemed to lift her higher and higher, taking her away from the fears she lived with and slept with day and night. Without even realizing what she was doing, she let go her trembling grip on the seat back and lifted her arms, allowing them to float winglike beside her, her palms held aloft by the icy rush of wind that howled by her ears and face. She felt weightless, totally separated from the wagon, drifting effortlessly across the meadow like the hawks in the mountains, like the clouds high overhead, like the great birds of her dreams. Closing her eyes, she imagined herself gliding among the trees, drifting over streams and rivers, leaping great canyons in effortless glee.

How she'd longed to feel such freedom, to experience movement without pain. Always she'd wanted to race around the bases at school, following the shouts of her classmates as she headed for home plate. She'd longed to speed up the never-ending staircases that faced her day after day and arrive at the top with breath to spare, to jump over sidewalks, to run just for the sake of running. Never had she been able to act like other kids her age who had healthy, fully functioning lungs. The past 12 months had been unrelenting agony as she'd felt the life forces in her chest draining away.

But right now the screaming wind and the headlong rush across the meadow pushed all of those thoughts, all of those fears and sadnesses and embarrassments, aside. For one delicious moment, she could run, she could jump, she could *fly!*

Joey glanced over at Wendy, whose gaze remained fixed on the girl's face. She smiled and nodded, her eyes encouraging the young wrangler to hold Tar Boy just a few more seconds at full run, allowing Emily to enjoy the sensations she was feeling a little longer. The boy obeyed, keeping the reins loose in his hands, watching the world flash by amid the thunder of hooves and surge of the wagon.

But even horses like Tar Boy have limits, and Joey and Wendy both knew that it was time to bring the experience to a close. Slowly, smoothly, the horse abated his headlong lunge across the autumn meadow, shifting from a full run to a gallop, from a gallop to a canter, from a canter to a trot, and finally settling comfortably into a fast walk, his thick, black coat shimmering with moisture in the sunlight.

As the rush of wind diminished, Wendy saw Emily's body relax, her shoulders drooping slightly as her arms fell back to her sides. When Tar Boy eased to a slow walk, she heard the girl crying softly, her face wet with tears.

Wendy stood and wrapped her arms around her friend, feeling the girl's quiet sobs rock her body. Had she made a mistake? Had the ride been too much for her? Had she hurt her friend terribly? Then Emily's arms encircled her and she heard a weak, frail voice whisper in her ear, "It was better than my dreams. Oh Wendy, you let me fly!"

Joey turned his face away, tears stinging his own eyes. Around them the meadow shone brightly in the cold afternoon sun and the sky hung deep blue overhead. The wagon had performed flawlessly, and he knew that the many hours he'd spent restoring it had been worth every second. *Every* second.

Night stars hung in the darkness like candles adorning the windows of a million distant cottages. Shadow Creek ran cold and silent beside the pasture, slipping under the footbridge and continuing down the valley unseen. Inside the Station, light from the flickering fireplace cast long shadows over the den, creating a mysterious warmth that brushed against the faces of those relaxing in its glow.

Wendy wrinkled her nose and studied the game board thoughtfully. If she moved her piece to the left, Grandpa Hanson would jump her best chance of getting a man crowned. But if she shifted it to the right, she'd place her backup pieces in jeopardy. Yet if she stayed where she was, he would most certainly begin an end-run around her guard and invade her home row in three moves. After that, her rear defenses would be toast.

"I never did like this game," Wendy mumbled, chin resting on a clenched fist, feet slowly fanning the air behind her prone body.

"You always say that when you're losing," Grandpa Hanson stated.

The girl frowned. "I'm not losing. I'm just . . . regrouping."

"You're losing," the old man repeated. "I've got you so hemmed in by my mighty warriors that if you tried to make an escape I'd eat you for supper."

"Shush, old man," Grandma Hanson called from her spot by the window. "It's just a game."

Her husband shook his head. "Yeah, like Everest is just a mountain. I've got her beat and she knows it."

Wendy pursed her lips slightly. "What if I did this?" she asked, motioning as if she was moving a piece forward.

"I'd get you in two moves."

"And this?" she continued, feigning another move on the other side of the board.

"I'd take out your left guard and your backup man," Grandpa Hanson smirked.

"Well, then, what if I moved this piece from here to here?"

The old man hesitated. "I'd . . . I'd do something terrible to it very shortly."

A grin creased her face. "Ah-ha! You didn't see that one, did you? You were so sure of yourself, so positive that you were going to wipe the ground with me that you forgot about my mighty warrior sitting over here minding his own business, just waiting for you to weaken. Well, my friend, my worthy enemy, my old but still cuddly grandfather, just watch this." With a flourish, Wendy pushed her red piece forward one square and smiled broadly. "This game is *not* finished. I am *not* defeated."

Wordlessly, Grandpa Hanson picked up a black piece and jumped three of her pieces.

Wendy blinked. "I'm finished. I'm defeated." She laid her head down on her folded arms. "I hate this game," she moaned.

The old man grinned as he rearranged the pieces on the board. "Wanna try for a best of seven? I'll go easy next time."

Her head jerked up. "Yes. *Yes!* Again to the front lines. Again to arms. The battle may be lost but the war—oh the war, it is far from over. Set them up again and prepare to feel the cold, heartless steel of defeat." She paused. "Want some popcorn?"

"Buttered. No salt."

The girl jumped up and ran toward the kitchen. As she passed Emily who was sitting by the bookcase with Feathers nestled in her lap, she grinned. "He's such a pussycat. If I get him munching on popcorn, he'll lose concentration. That's when I'll nail his hide to the wall!"

Emily grinned. "Go get 'em, tiger," she called.

Feathers lifted his head and looked around. He too had smelled the corn popping in some distant corner of the Station. It reminded him of warm days spent in a land far from this valley, where among cornfields he'd felt the summer sun touch and soothe his feathers like a gentle breeze.

His strength was returning slowly, although it still hurt to move his legs and wings. By now, his fear of people had lessened greatly, replaced by a strange, incomprehensible trust. Humans had always been the one species his kind had feared the most. They could hurt you in ways unimaginable, pick you right out of the sky and send you plunging to your death. He'd seen it happen many times.

But here, surrounding him, were humans who didn't have death on their minds, creatures who touched him with gentleness and kindness, bringing him food and providing a soft shelter in which to hide. Even their voices sounded harmless as they mumbled and whispered words he didn't understand.

The duck glanced up at Emily. This creature, like the one with the golden plumage, seemed especially kind, stroking his bent and broken feathers endlessly, showering him with attention and tasty things to eat. Maybe the flock had been wrong to fear humans. Perhaps those that tore his kind from the sky were different, not as advanced as these. Maybe, just maybe, those who brought death weren't even human at all.

Emily sighed as she continued to run the back of her fingers over the soft curve of the mallard's neck. "You're getting better, aren't you?" she said softly. "You look healthier. Even your eyes shine a little brighter than before. Soon you'll be flying away, heading south to catch up with your family.

Well, I don't blame you. They probably miss you and have been looking in every pond and river for you, wondering why you're not around anymore."

Emily rested her head against the leg of the small table rising by her side. "Just be patient," she whispered. "Just wait a little longer and you'll fly again. You'll see. You'll flap your wings and off you'll go, across the forests and meadows and mountains, flying higher and higher until you find your family and can travel with them again. That's what you want most, isn't it? That's what you dream about. I know it is."

Wendy reentered the den, balancing bowls of popcorn in her outstretched arms. "Here, Emily," she called. "This one's for you and Feathers. The one in the green bowl is Grandpa's, and mine's red." Emily accepted the offered container piled high with freshly popped kernels. "Now, if you'll excuse me, there's a war to be won."

As her friend scurried across the room and took up her position at one end of the checkers board on the floor by the fireplace, Emily heard someone call her name. She glanced up as Ms. Cadena settled in beside her, a bowl of popcorn cupped in her hands. Outside, beyond the tall windows fronting the den, the stars continued their silent journey across the sky.

"How'd your wagon ride go this afternoon?" the woman asked. "Joey said you guys had a lot of fun."

Emily grinned broadly. "Oh, we did! It was

great. We went clear to the top of a mountain and it was *so* beautiful. I've never seen anything like it in my whole life."

Ruth Cadena smiled. "I'm glad you had a good time. The Hansons are wonderful people and love it when teens come out to the ranch for a visit. They want you to return as often as you'd like. In fact, they've even named the room you're staying in as 'Emily's Room.' It's yours for the whole winter."

The girl beamed. "Wow. That's really neat."

The woman's expression turned more serious. "I was at the hospital today. One of my kids bummed up his knee pretty bad. After I made sure he was going to be OK, I had a talk with your doctor."

Emily's smile faded. "You did?"

"Yeah. He, uh, he said he wants you to come in for a few more tests."

"That bad, huh?" The girl lowered her eyes.

"I'm afraid it is. He said you're not responding to the medication and wants to try some other drugs and stuff. I'm sorry, Emily. I wish I could tell you good news instead. I stopped by and spoke with your parents and brought them up-to-date."

"I wish you hadn't done that."

"Why?"

The girl sighed. "I cause them enough grief as it is. I've spent all their money, wiped out their savings. Dad can't even fix the car because of my stupid hospital bills."

"Emily, they're not worried about that. They just want to help you get well."

"Mom and Dad can't even go out on a date anymore. They can't eat at a restaurant or go someplace romantic. They have to stay around and take care of me when they're not working their heads off. I hate it."

Ms. Cadena leaned forward. "They don't mind, Emily. They love you. You're their daughter."

"Yeah, well, I'm also the jerk who makes their life miserable. They'd be better off without me."

"*No!* No, they wouldn't! Your mother and father adore you, bad lungs and all. They told me that they can't stand having you away for the weekend because they miss you so much and are counting the hours until you get home after school on Monday. In fact, they're even planning a welcome home party that night with a cake and everything. Emily, your parents love you very much."

The girl stared out the dark window for a long moment. "I hear my mother crying at night because she's so tired from working two jobs. My dad can't help her because he's totally zonked out from his 12 hours at the industrial park cleaning toilets. That's what he does, you know. He cleans toilets and mops floors because he can't get any other job and he can't get any other job because he doesn't have a car that runs. And why doesn't he have a car? Because he's paying doctor bills and lab bills and medicine bills for me, that's why."

The social worker turned the girl's face with her hand and stared into her eyes. "It doesn't matter, Emily. They don't look at it that way. Just this afternoon, your father asked if there was something else they could do, some piece of equipment they could buy, that would help you breathe better. Love doesn't operate only when everything's going well, when lungs are healthy and bodies are free from disease. True love kicks into gear when tears flow and hearts break. Your parents aren't worried about the money they don't have for an outing to Taco Bell. They're far more concerned that you're getting the best care possible. And," the woman hesitated, "that care may be in Chicago."

"Chicago?"

"Yeah. Your doctor suggested that it might be time to take you over there for some more tests. They've got better instruments and more up-to-date procedures, to say nothing of experts in respiratory care. Maybe you and your parents should check it out."

Emily shook her head. "But that costs money."

"Let us worry about that," Ms. Cadena said. "We've made it so far, haven't we?"

"I guess so."

"Then we'll find a way in Chicago too. You've got more friends than you know, Emily."

The girl nodded slowly. "But . . ."

"But what?"

Turning, Emily stared through the window to

the dark forms blotting out the horizon, their summits fingering the stars. "I can't go to Chicago," she whispered.

"Why? Why, Emily?"

She remained silent for a long moment. Ms. Cadena studied her face, trying to catch a hint of the emotions raging within the girl. In the past Emily had always been open to any thread of hope, any plan centered on a new treatment or drug that might ease her relentless pain and debilitating condition. She'd welcomed them with firm resolve, believing each time that finally her battle would be over, that she would gain a normal life in which breathing wasn't a struggle and the future was waiting bright and hopeful just around the corner. But this time, Ruth Cardena saw no such determination or feeling of purpose. The girl had only silence and a terrible emptiness to her expression.

Emily closed her eyes, as if reviewing something in her thoughts, as if she saw some vision more meaningful than the words she and the social worker were exchanging. "I can't go to Chicago," she said, "because in the city . . . there aren't any mountains."

She glanced at Ms. Cadena for just a moment, then let her gaze fall on the sleeping duck.

The woman's heart suddenly felt heavy and afraid. She'd seen that look before. It had been on the face of a young boy she'd held in her arms as his life had slipped away, the result of a self-inflicted gunshot wound.

CHAPTER 5

Kidnapped!

Sunday morning stirred gray and foreboding as the sun slipped unseen from behind the mountains to the east, creating only a faint glow to mark its rise. During the night storm clouds had marched through the valley, depositing a thick carpet of snow on every forest glen and pine-bordered meadow, transforming the world, removing all color from its upturned face.

Emily sat by the still-glowing embers of last evening's fire, staring out through one of the den windows at the bleak half-light of dawn, listening to the sounds of the Station as those who called it home drifted from sleep into consciousness. Wendy had just stopped by on her way to the front door, looking like a comical cloth monster under layer upon layer of clothes. "Gotta check on Early," she'd said, her voice muffled by the scarves wrapped tightly about her face. "He likes an extra helping of oats on Sunday morning. Besides, he doesn't like snowstorms. I've gotta calm him down a bit."

Emily had nodded and smiled, knowing that she couldn't follow her new friend through the drifts. The effort would be far more than she could endure. She also understood that it wasn't necessarily Early who felt unsettled by the passing storm. Stories that had echoed about the hearth the night before had recalled another time, another moment in Shadow Creek Ranch history, when a deadly blizzard had caught the Hansons and several of their friends in a terrifying grip, forcing some of them to the very edge of survival. No, Wendy hadn't been afraid of the storm that passed during the night. She'd been frightened by the memories that whispered in its winds.

The girl watched her classmate struggle through knee-high drifts, leaving a crumbling wake behind her as she moved slowly away from the broad porch in the direction of the footbridge.

"Let me guess," someone called, startling Emily. "She's worried about Early, so she's risking frostbite to go from this warm house to that cold barn to make sure he's OK."

Joey sat down in the big chair by the frost-framed window and peered into the gray world beyond. "I told her that mule of hers was fine. But does she listen to me? Noooo! She has to trudge out there through the snow to see for herself. That's one stubborn dame."

Emily giggled. "She loves Early. That's why she's doing it."

He nodded. "Yeah. I know. But I gotta complain about her. It's part of my job description."

The boy pulled his thick bathrobe tighter about him, trying to ward off the early-morning chill. "I suppose you want a fire in there," he said, pointing at the fading embers in the big hearth.

She shrugged. "Would be nice. Is that in your job description too?"

"*Everything* is," he chuckled as he stumbled to his feet. "Actually, Debbie is the best fire builder in the family. She can make one that's really pretty, you know, with the front logs burning and flickering like you see in movies or magazine pictures with a man and woman sitting on a rug drinking hot chocolate and gazing into each other's eyes like two nearsighted optometrists. I don't know how she does it." Kneeling by the hearth, he started collecting kindling from the bin resting nearby. "Now me, I can build a fire that'll make you sweat buckets. Heats up the whole house. But it looks more like a furnace than a movie prop. Guess I don't have that special touch."

"You sure have a special touch with horses," Emily said. "They do exactly what you tell 'em to do."

Joey nodded. "They just know who's boss, that's all. And I give them treats from time to time. Guess they don't wanna bite the hand that feeds 'em. Smart critters."

Emily watched him crumple sheets of newspaper, then arrange a small, neat pile of split logs over the top of them. She noticed that the boy hummed softly to himself as he worked.

After a few moments the girl broke the stillness. "You found it, didn't you?"

Joey blinked. "Found what?"

For a moment she glanced out the window at the gray dawn. "That planet of joy Pastor Webley was talking about yesterday. You found it right here at Shadow Creek Ranch."

The young wrangler paused in his work as he tried to recall the enthusiastic minister's words. "Oh, yeah. I guess I have. Beats living in New York City, that's for sure. I'll take a blizzard over a mugging any day."

Emily was quiet for a long moment. "You're lucky," she said finally.

Joey blew gently on the embers, igniting the paper almost instantly. "I am lucky," he responded, sitting back on his heels as the dry kindling began to crackle. "But luck's a funny thing. I know guys who love the city. Wouldn't leave it for the world. They'd hate Montana with its mountains and rivers and horse manure. Instead, they feel lucky right where they are. Put them on a working ranch in the middle of the Gallatin National Forest and they'd be miserable.

Of course, I think they're absolutely bonkers."

The girl sighed. "I don't know how to find it. You must gotta have lots of breath to live there, and breath isn't exactly something I've got a lot of."

"Maybe, maybe not," Joey said softly, stirring the kindling with a metal poker. "I don't believe breathing is the most important thing in this case. Maybe *thinking* is. You gotta *think* you've got it made even if other people don't agree, like some of my buddies back in New York. They actually feel sorry for me out here in the wilderness with no cable TV or fast-food restaurants or other fancy city stuff. 'Poor Dugan,' they say. 'He's living a miserable life.' And I'm out here on the ranch feeling sorry for them at the same time."

She leaned forward. "So you're saying that people can make any place a planet of joy?"

Joey frowned. "Well, yeah, I guess I am. It really isn't a place, I suppose. It's more of an attitude or a choice you make." He glanced about the softly lit den. "Some choices are easier to make than others. I think I was born to live on Shadow Creek Ranch. Heaven's gonna be just like this, but without all the death and pain. I won't be running down any ducks with my truck."

With a grin Emily glanced over at the cardboard box resting by the bookcase. "I think ol' Feathers would like heaven too," she said.

Joey stood and walked to the far wall. "How is our little friend today?" he asked, pulling back the soft blanket covering the container. "He looks pretty good to me."

The animal stirred and glanced up at his early-morning visitor.

"Hi guy," Joey said.

Feathers quacked sharply and tucked his head back under his wing. The wrangler flinched. "I think he knows I was driving the truck," he whispered, replacing the blanket and smoothing out the wrinkles. "Maybe I'd better just leave him alone."

Emily shook her head. "He forgives you. I know he does."

Joey frowned. "He looked kinda mad if you ask me. Let's just say I won't be getting an invitation for his next family reunion down in Florida this Christmas. They'll probably have my picture tacked up on a tree and throw darts at it."

The girl burst out laughing, then composed herself, working to control her breathing. "Oh, you're just being silly. They all know it was an accident."

He nodded. "I sure hope so 'cause I love animals, even ones with feathers." Then he paused. "And speaking of animals, I'd better get out to the barn before Wendy overfeeds the entire herd. She thinks dumping oats down them will make them stronger and faster. Well, in the winter months all that eating only makes them fatter." Joey turned and hurried from the den. "See ya later," he called over his shoulder.

Emily waved and sighed as deeply as her lungs would allow. It would be so easy to believe in a planet called joy if you lived on Shadow Creek Ranch. But out there, beyond the den's warm embrace, were endless storms and days and nights filled with pain and uncertainty. Perhaps Pastor Webley and Joey were wrong. Maybe there existed hidden places unseen by others where joy could never find a foothold. Most discouraging of all to the young girl sitting by the window listening to the fire crackle at her feet was the thought that it might be possible that she was forever destined to live in one of them.

Closing her eyes, Emily envisioned a hawk flying freely over the mountaintops, far from the choking snowdrifts, far from the hidden places, far from the painful presence of reality.

The hallway of the Lewis and Clark Elementary School fairly trembled under the wet, snowy tread of dozens of noisy students. Overhead, the morning bell clanged, announcing that in five minutes another chime would remind everyone that they should be sitting quietly in their classrooms. A feeling of familiarity about the chaotic scene left Emily strangely comforted. It was loud, it was breezy, and it was Monday morning.

Wendy exited the registrar's office with an amazed expression spread across her face. "What happened?" Emily asked as her friend joined her by the lockers.

"You're not going to believe this," Wendy stated, "but as of now, Feathers is officially, legally, and totally registered at this school. He's in first grade, has his own lunch ticket, an 'I LOVE LEWIS & CLARK' notebook, a box of new pencils courtesy of the office supply store at the Bozeman mall, and a sheet of instructions on how to get his picture taken for the yearbook."

"You're kidding."

"No, I'm not. I even said to the woman, 'Listen, ma'am, I need for you to understand something important. Feathers is a duck. A *duck.*' She didn't even look up from her work. Chuckling, she just said, 'That's all right. For the first seven years of his life, my nephew thought he was a goat.'" The girl spread her hands. "What am I supposed to do now?"

They looked at each other, then at the box at their feet. Slowly, they knelt and pulled back the cover. "Feathers," they chorused, "welcome to Lewis and Clark." With that pronouncement formally delivered, they stood and joined the current of young people as it flowed toward their classroom. The school's newest first grader peered at the world from his open box. He seemed proud of his new standing in life.

Miss Elrod smiled down at her students as the second bell rattled from the emptying hallway. "Good morning, all," she called. "I see everyone

made it through the first storm of the season OK."
Wendy noticed the woman's hair was no longer
pulled back from her face and held in place by stiff
combs, but now lay soft on her narrow shoulders,
giving her a much kinder, approachable appearance. "I was snowbound for a time," the instructor
declared, "but my new neighbor, Mr. Anderson
from Seattle, came over and shoveled my driveway for me. It's nice to have a neighbor who's so
handsome with a shovel." Miss Elrod paused, her
face suddenly flushed. "Did I say handsome? I
meant handy. Mr. Anderson is handy with a muscle. I mean *shovel!*"

Wendy glanced at Emily and rolled her eyes.
Her friend suppressed a giggle with her fingers
and blinked as if portraying a damsel in distress.

The teacher leaned against her desk, trying to
regain her composure. "So . . . uh . . . I see everyone made it through the first storm of the season
OK," she repeated, a little out of breath. "That's
. . . fine. Good. Now we must get to work. We can
discuss the storm later."

Everyone in the room reached for their geography book and exchanged knowing glances. The
short-lived blizzard had done more damage than
they'd imagined. Apparently, it had knocked the
combs right out of Miss Elrod's hair.

For the first time since joining the ranks of the
student body at Lewis and Clark, Wendy felt like
she belonged. The classroom had a warmth she

hadn't noticed before, a kind of friendliness that drifted with the hum of activity and buzz of voices as knowledge was being dispensed and absorbed. No, it wasn't as nice as the den on Shadow Creek Ranch, and Miss Elrod was certainly no Lizzy Pierce, but there was something to be said about going to school with a few hundred other young people. A weird type of security came with being jammed in a room with other students her age while snow covered the parking lot and playground beyond the windows.

Wendy looked over at Emily and nodded slowly to herself. Now she knew why she felt that way. She had a friend. For some reason, it made all the difference in the world.

Sensing someone staring at her, Wendy allowed her gaze to drift a little more to the right. Her eyes met two others set within a scowling, slightly puffy face ringed with brown curly hair and a receding chin. Oh yes. The school did have one unfortunate flaw that didn't seem to go away. Among the student body was a sixth grader with a problem. His name was Garwin Huffinger. And she seemed to be his problem.

The boy held her gaze as he lifted his finger and pointed at the box by the bookcase. Then he drew his hand past his throat as if slicing his neck with a knife. Wendy felt her own hands tighten about her geography book. She looked away quickly, not wanting to give him the satisfaction of knowing

116

that she'd noticed or understood the meaning of his gesture. Before returning to her studies, the girl slipped a quick glance at the box. Feathers stood with his head held just above the top of the container, watching the activity that swirled about him. Her eyes narrowed. Not only was Garwin threatening her injured friend Emily, he was also acting unkindly toward Lewis and Clark's newest fully registered first grader. Wendy would tolerate neither. She knew she'd have to deal with Garwin Huffinger again—probably very, very soon.

Unlike the mornings she'd endured during her first week at the new school, today sped by quickly for Wendy, her mind bouncing between South America, old English literature, fractions, and space travel. She was even surprised when the dinner bell clanked in the hallway.

As Grandma Hanson put it, it was time to get some "fuel for the body pumped in one spoonful at a time." Today's fuel of choice was tacos and burritos smothered with hot sauce and ringed with salty chips. Wendy and Emily stood in line with their classmates, waiting for the surprisingly skinny cook who stood at the serving table to dish out the food onto their plates.

The man smiled broadly as the two sixth graders approached. "And how about you young ladies?" he asked warmly. "One or two burritos?"

"One," Emily responded.

"Three," Wendy announced.

"I'm sorry," the cook said. "I'm only allowed to serve either one or two burritos on each tray."

Emily frowned. "Well, then, I changed my mind. I'll take two. But I don't want my plate to get so full that everything mixes together, so would you kindly put one of my burritos on my friend's plate? She doesn't mind her food getting all mixed up, and she can keep my second burrito safe and sound for me."

The man nodded. "Of course. I'll just . . ." He paused and stared at Wendy. "That means you'll have three burritos on your plate, but you're only allowed two."

"Hey, one of those will be hers," Wendy replied. "So, officially, you're only giving me two burritos. I'm just carrying that other one for her. How many tacos can we have?"

"Two each."

"Great. But I think I'd better carry all of my friend's tacos for her because, as she said, she doesn't like it when her food gets mixed up, so just put them here on my tray and we'll work everything out later. Do you have chocolate milk?"

The cook frowned. "Chocolate milk with Mexican food?"

Wendy nodded. "Mexicans like chocolate. I have this friend, Miss Cadena, and do you know what her favorite ice cream is?"

"Chocolate?"

"Well, no, her favorite is strawberry, but once we were at Charlie's in Bozeman and they were out of strawberry, so do you know what she chose?"

"Chocolate?"

"Not exactly. She got fudge ripple but, as you know, it has chocolate in it. Miss Cadena sat right there in front of me and ate it. A genuine Mexican eating chocolate. It really happened. You can ask my dad."

The cook stared at Wendy for a long moment, then wordlessly fished around in the small cooler at his elbow and withdrew a carton of chocolate milk.

"I'll have one of those too," Emily declared, smiling sweetly.

The cook repeated his search and retrieved another carton from the cooler. He was about to place it on Emily's tray when Wendy cleared her throat. With a tired nod, he dropped the second carton on her tray and waved the two girls away.

"Thank you, sir," Wendy said. "Everything looks delicious. Really it does." The man didn't answer. He was too busy studying Wendy's tray piled high with three burritos, four tacos, and two cartons of chocolate milk.

"Oh, by the way," the girl added, "may I have some extra chips? I love chips and . . ."

The cook fixed her with a cold stare.

"Never mind." She and Emily backed away

from the counter. "This will be fine. Yeah. This is great. Thanks. Goodbye."

They hurried out of the cafeteria, casting nervous glances over their shoulders. A minute later they settled in at their desks. Between chews, Wendy stated, "I coulda got more sauce, but I didn't want to press my luck."

Emily nodded, slowly enjoying the single burrito adorning her plate.

The two friends suppressed their giggles while enjoying their meal.

Before long, Emily had picked her plate clean and Wendy's dishes looked like they'd passed through a dishwasher. "I *love* Mexican," Wendy breathed, rubbing her somewhat bulging tummy. "But this still isn't as good as Ms. Cadena's burritos. That woman can do stuff with flour and refried beans that would make a conquistador cry like a baby."

Emily nodded. "Tomorrow we're having Chinese. I think the cook's on an international kick. Get ready for lots of noodles and eggs."

Her companion patted her stomach again. "I'll be ready. My dad can't believe how much I eat. Says I must be hollow inside. Mr. Dugan insists that all my food goes to my head 'cause there's lots of empty space for storage up there. He's a regular comic."

Emily giggled, then pointed at the covered box. "Hey, we didn't leave anything for Feathers."

"Not to fear," Wendy stated, reaching into her

desk and withdrawing a slip of paper. "Duck has got his own meal ticket, remember? I'll just go and get his food for him."

"Ah, maybe I'd better do that," Emily said, stumbling to her feet. "That cook will be on the lookout for you. If you ask for more food, *you'll* be the main course tomorrow."

"Yeah, I guess you're right," Wendy agreed, handing the meal ticket to her friend. "Get lots of salad stuff and bread. I don't think beans would suit a duck's taste buds."

"OK. I'll be right back."

As Emily walked to the door, Wendy leaned over and tugged on the blanket covering the box. "Hey, Feathers, you hungr—" The word froze in her throat. Emily glanced around just as her friend jumped to her feet. "It's empty," Wendy breathed. "He's gone." She looked wildly about the room, then at her friend. "Someone has stolen Feathers!"

Garwin Huffinger was sitting alone at the farthest table in the cafeteria when he suddenly found himself surrounded by two angry classmates. "What'd you do with him?" Emily asked.

"Him who?"

"Him. Feathers. Our duck!"

The boy frowned. "I killed him, cooked him, and now I'm eating him for lunch."

Wendy snatched the food from the boy's hand

and ripped it open. "Don't say that," she commanded, examining the contents of the half-eaten burrito. "There's nothing in here but beans and onions. Where's Feathers?"

"You guys are crazy," he stated, grabbing back his lunch. "That stupid bird doesn't belong in a school for people. He should be in a zoo or a stew. Now leave me alone."

"Not until you tell us where you hid him," Wendy continued. "This isn't funny. That animal is hurt and needs to be fed right now."

Garwin grinned. "Well, well. You do like that duck, don't you?" He leaned back in his chair and intertwined his fingers behind his head. "What's he worth to you?"

"What do you mean, what's he worth?"

"How much would you pay to have him back?"

Wendy leaned over the boy, almost causing him to fall out of his chair. "I might let you live," she said coldly.

Garwin shook his head. "I sense a lot of hostility coming from you today. May I suggest some therapy might be in order?"

Wendy's right fist tightened along with her stomach. She held her position over Garwin, not exactly sure what to do next. All of her life she'd responded to such situations with decided action, attacking her problems physically when necessary. But here, away from the safety and support of the big Station in the valley, she was on her own. Not only that, she was supposed to be a Christian. She was supposed to be different, to act different, to talk different. Grandpa Hanson had told her that life would contain people who would watch her, waiting to see if she had the ability to live her convictions.

She edged closer to the sweating boy, her eyes locked on his. All those sermons, all those late-night talks with her dad, all those confrontations with Joey were supposed to teach her something important, to prepare her to face the Garwin Huffingers of the world. But she didn't feel like a Christian right now. Nor did she feel like being nice and forgiving and tolerant and kind. Instead, she felt like punching the boy's lights out, and she could do it. She knew that. But what would that prove? That she was the better bully? That she could flatten an overweight jerk with one swing of her ranch-hardened arm? Oh sure, that would get Feathers back really fast.

Wendy withdrew slowly, her gaze still frozen on his face. "Five dollars," she breathed. "I'll give you $5."

"Twenty," Garwin said.

"I don't have $20," Wendy retorted, her words measured and even.

"Then you're out of luck." The boy lowered his chair onto all four legs and adjusted the napkin jammed in his shirt. "Now, if you'll excuse me, I've got a lunch to finish. Come up with the cash, I'll give you your bird."

Wendy and Emily looked at each other, sighed with frustration, then walked slowly out of the cafeteria. When they were in the hallway, Emily spoke quietly. "What're we gonna do? Garwin might hurt Feathers, or keep his promise to do even worse. Oh, Wendy, what're we gonna do?" Tears began to sting her eyes as she spoke.

Wendy remained silent for a long moment. Finally she said, "*We're* not going to do anything. Feathers is."

"What do you mean?"

"You'll see."

Returning to the classroom, they lowered themselves onto their desk chairs. Emily frowned and studied her friend's face. What was Feathers going to do that would enable them to find him? She closed her eyes. More important, if Wendy's idea didn't work, what was she going to do without the duck?

While the morning had sped by almost without notice, the afternoon slowed to a crawl. Wendy couldn't concentrate, no matter how hard she tried. She kept glancing in the direction of Garwin's desk, eyeing him thoughtfully, trying to keep her anger in check.

She'd even considered telling Miss Elrod what had happened, but thought better of it. Adults certainly had their place in the world. But in her mind, some things were better left in the hands of those who had a vested interest in the situation. The last thing she wanted was a roomful of laughing sixth graders running all over the school looking for her bird. While it was bad enough to bring a duck to school, it was another matter to lose it to someone like Garwin.

Wendy looked at Emily. The girl wasn't doing so well. She'd formed a powerful bond with the creature, a connection of shared pain and a feeling of hopelessness. Wendy knew that wild animals, even injured ones, could withstand a lot of rough treatment at the hands of human beings. After all, Feathers had been blindsided by a truck and survived. He could probably defend himself against the likes of Garwin Huffinger, at least if things didn't get too far out of hand. But Emily was a different story. She wasn't as strong. Her injury was deeper, affecting not only her body but her mind as well. Wendy didn't understand everything that was going on in Emily's world, but she knew enough. They had better find that duck, and it had better be soon.

By the time the final bell rang, the two girls had about reached the end of their patience. Garwin had made no attempt to return the creature or reveal where he'd hidden it. Feathers wasn't in the classroom, that was for sure. They'd searched every place big enough to hold their bird while trying to go about their studies and not draw attention to themselves. Now, Wendy was counting on one fact that she believed would reveal where Garwin had hidden the missing animal. Feathers had been kidnapped at the beginning of the lunch break while she and Emily were in line getting their burritos. It meant that the animal, whose appetite had been growing by leaps and bounds during the past two days, hadn't eaten since breakfast. What Garwin Huffinger didn't know was that a hungry duck was a grouchy duck and, hopefully, a noisy one as well.

After waving goodbye to her students, Miss Elrod headed immediately for the parking lot. It seemed she had an appointment that afternoon with someone who was both handsome and able to shovel tall driveways with a single bound. As Garwin exited the classroom with the other students, he suddenly discovered that he had a two-girl escort.

"Leave me alone," he ordered, pausing in the hallway.

"Give us back our duck," Wendy countered coldly.

"You got the money?"

"Nope."

"Then you can kiss your stupid critter goodbye."

"I'm not going to kiss anything, much less a duck," she retorted. "We just thought we'd follow you around for a while. You're such a warm, wonderful person that we can't help being attracted to you. We're drawn to you like butterflies to a cow pie."

"Very funny," Garwin declared with a shove. "But it's not going to do you any good. The duck isn't even here."

"Oh?" Wendy responded, falling in again beside the fast-walking boy. "Whad'ya do, FedEx him to Florida where he belongs?"

"Just leave me alone!" Garwin demanded. "I don't like you following me around like this. The guys will start talking."

"Yeah? What about?"

"About you following me around. I hate girls— all girls—and you are girls, both of you."

"Thanks for noticing," Emily said, her breathing becoming a little labored as she fought to keep up.

Garwin stopped and held up his hand. "Look. I've gotta get home, so *bug off!*"

Wendy nodded. "OK. OK. We'll stop. But just remember, we warned you."

"Fine. Great. Now *leave me alone!*"

The boy started down the hallway when he suddenly stopped and turned. "Warned me about what?" Wendy and Emily were nowhere to be seen. They'd disappeared in the throng of students scurrying by.

"Warned me. Yeah, right," Garwin said under his breath. "They don't know what they're talking about."

When he reached his locker, which was located about midsection in the long passageway, he paused and looked first one way and then another. Yes, the two girls were nowhere in sight. Bending low, he studied the numbers on his combination lock. First he twisted the knob to the left, then to the right, then back to the left again. With one final, nervous glance up and down the hallway, Garwin pulled the door open a crack and peeked inside.

The locker seemed to explode in a cloud of dust, notebook paper, discarded candy wrappers, and feathers. Garwin saw what looked like a thick arrow with a beak shoot from the top shelf and slam into his forehead, sending him reeling into a group of astonished classmates. He felt powerful wings pummel his nose and chin before beating him mercilessly about the shoulders while an ear-splitting racket of squawks and quacks roared in his ears. Then his attacker disappeared as quickly as he'd appeared, leaving Garwin gasping for breath.

Wendy and Emily, who'd been hiding just around the corner from the locker, watched in amazement as Feathers, finally freed from his dark metal cell, blasted past them, half running, half flying as he shot down the hallway, sending students diving for cover amid screams and shouts.

The animal finally lifted himself off the ground on unsteady wings and ricocheted his way toward the wide front doors guarding the far end of the long, broad passageway. He would have made good his escape except that, at the last moment, the registrar burst from her office to see what all the commotion was about. Wendy screamed,

"Watch out!" but it was too late. In the next instant, the fast-moving duck and horrified woman slammed into each other, the impact sending them and several students sprawling across the smooth, polished tiles just inside the exit. The woman wound up in a crumpled pile in the corner with Feathers sitting on her chest, quacking loudly into her fear-contorted face.

Wendy and Emily rushed past the prone figures of their classmates and skidded to a stop over the disheveled mess that moments ago had been Lewis and Clark's highly professional registrar. "Are you all right?" Wendy asked, hurriedly retrieving the squawking duck and passing him on to Emily. "Are you hurt? Should I call a doctor or something?"

The woman tried to straighten her now-smudged and twisted blazer. "What was that awful monster that attacked me?" she gasped, looking about with a terrified expression. "It was horrible! I came out into the hall and before I could do anything, it was on me, beating me, yelling into my face."

"Well, to be totally factual, it wasn't yelling," Wendy corrected, helping the trembling woman to her feet. "It was quacking . . . like a duck." She pointed at Emily. "Like *that* duck." The registrar stared at the animal now resting peacefully in Emily's arms. "He didn't mean to hurt you," Wendy continued. "He was just trying to escape Garwin Huffinger, who had kidnapped him and held him for ransom in his locker, which, I might add, is against the law."

"Kidnapped? Escape? Against the law?" the woman sputtered.

"I'm really sorry about all this," Wendy stated, brushing down from the woman's hair. "You have every right to be upset. Here, let me help you back to your office where you can . . . can do something like write a report on your typewriter. We'll just get Feathers out of your way so you won't have any more trouble, OK?" Even before she finished the sentence, Wendy flinched, realizing what she had just given away.

The registrar nodded. "Yes. My office." Then she paused. "Feathers?"

Wendy tightened her grip on the woman's elbow and began walking a little faster. "Don't think about this right now. You've had a bad accident. Not every day you get run down in a hallway by a duck, huh? That must've been awful. Just awful. Let's get you back in your office before anything else bad happens."

"Feathers?" the registrar repeated.

"Now there you go reliving the terrible accident again," Wendy warned, opening the office door. "Mustn't do that. You come in here and sit down . . . or file something. You'll feel better really fast. Honest. Just put the whole thing out of your mind."

"Where have I heard that name before?" the woman breathed.

"You hear so many names. It's easy to get them mixed up. There, you look much better now. I've gotta go. You just rest for a while. Sharpen a pencil or something. 'Bye."

"Have a nice day," the woman said weakly.

Hurrying from the room, Wendy found Emily still standing by the front exit, holding the duck. "Let's get outta here," she whispered, motioning for her friend to follow her down the hallway. "We've gotta get Feathers in his box and away from the school right now. The registrar is about to put two and two together and when she does, we're in big trouble. Let's get our coats and *go!*"

Slowing her pace, Emily called, "Wait. Did you see it? Did you see what Feathers did?"

"Yeah, he dive-bombed the registrar of the Lewis and Clark Elementary School."

"No. Just before that. He . . . he . . ."

"Yeah," Wendy grinned. "I saw. Neat, huh? Ol' Feathers is getting better and better."

Emily looked down at the bird. "He can fly." Then she looked up, sudden fear shadowing her face. "He can fly."

"Well, he *is* a duck."

"I know, but now . . ." The girl paused.

Wendy waved her hand. "Come on, Emily, we can talk about this later. Let's get out to the parking lot *now*. Joey should be waiting for us."

With a nod Emily followed her. But she didn't hurry. Her tread was slow and hesitant. What she'd seen had hit her almost as hard as the duck had struck the registrar. Feathers could not only eat and quack, he could do something more wonderful, more frightening. He could fly.

CHAPTER 6

Fly Away

Joey shook his head and chuckled. After a few moments, he did it again. Wendy glanced at him and smiled shyly. "It was kinda funny."

"Kinda?" the boy laughed. "I just wish I could've been there. I mean, it's not every day you get to watch a duck beat up a bully and then dive-bomb a school registrar." He changed gears and pressed on the accelerator, propelling the old truck along the highway at a little faster clip. "So, tell me again why this Garwin creep stole the bird?"

Wendy sighed. "Who knows. He's just a jerk with a bad attitude. Guess he wasn't getting enough attention from the rest of the school, so he decided to bother Emily and me for a while. Boy, he made me mad, too."

"You? Mad? That's never happened before."

The girl grinned.

"So," Joey continued, "where's Feathers now? How come he's not going back to the ranch with us?"

Wendy glanced out the window. "Emily was kinda freaked out about what happened at school, so I asked her if she wanted to keep Feathers overnight at her house. You should have seen how excited she got. Thought she'd jump right out of her skin. Her bus had just pulled away when you got there and rescued me from the future wrath of the registrar, which I'm sure is not going to be a pretty sight. I don't wanna be in the same county with her when she suddenly realizes she signed up a duck for first grade."

Joey laughed again. "How do you do it?" he asked.

"Do what?"

"Get yourself into so much trouble? If you're not being thrown off a mountain by a horse or getting caught in a snowstorm in a house with no electricity or falling headfirst into a hole in the ground, you're busy supervising the education of a waterfowl. What's next? An earthquake? Or maybe you'll get hit by lightning!"

Wendy shook her head. "I don't know why weird things happen to me all the time. Guess it's just nature's way of making up for the boring life you lead."

He smiled. "Boring's fine with me. You can have all the adventures. I'll be happy to stay on Shadow Creek Ranch forever and live a perfectly sane, uninteresting, run-of-the-mill life."

Suddenly, Wendy pointed. "Oh, can we stop there for a minute?"

They were just about to pass the little country church that the ranch family attended each Sabbath. Joey could see a familiar car parked by the front door and footprints leading from the vehicle up the steps to the entrance. "I don't think Webley does confessions on Monday afternoons," he said, guiding his truck into the parking lot, "but he might make an exception in your case."

His passenger rolled her eyes. "Very funny, Mr. Dugan. I just wanna talk to him for a minute." As soon as the truck slid to a stop on the freshly packed snow, she slipped out of the seat. "I think I hear Mrs. Webley practicing the organ. You wanna come in and listen? I won't be long."

"Sure," Joey agreed, unbuckling his seat belt. "But if I burst out singing, it's your fault."

Wendy paused. "Maybe you'd better wait in the car."

"Come on," he chuckled, "I'll keep it down just for you. Besides, I smell wood smoke. They've got the stove lit up. The heater in my truck isn't all that great as you probably already know."

The two stumbled up the steps and entered the small, dimly lit foyer. The rich, full tones of the organ wrapped around the new arrivals like strong, welcoming arms. Joey headed directly into the little sanctuary while Wendy walked down a flight of steps to the basement office of her friend Pastor Webley. She knocked gently on the door.

"I have a visitor?" a voice called out.

"It's me, Wendy."

"Wendy who?"

The girl grinned. "Cold, tired, and I-have-another-question Wendy."

"Oh her. The girl with the duck. Come right in."

Entering the small office, Wendy smiled at the man seated at a computer by the desk. Bookshelves lined the walls of the room. Where there were no books, she saw trinkets and figurines, all with a decidedly religious theme, such as the clay oil lamp from Israel, a crown of thorns fashioned from a prickly bush that grows in Arizona, and a handmade leather sling similar to the one David might have used to kill the giant.

Pastor Webley finished the sentence he was typing, then swung around in his chair. "Have a seat," he invited, pointing at a faded couch resting by a scale model of the sanctuary in the desert, a creation he had built with his own hands. It was his pride and joy.

"You like my new altar of burnt offerings?" he asked, pointing. "I think a mouse ate the old one. Who knew I was building a tasty model?"

Wendy admired the small structure resting in the courtyard of the meticulously constructed visual aid. "Nice," she said.

The man sighed. "Eighteen hours I work on that altar and all I get is nice?"

The girl blinked. "*Very* nice?"

"Ah. That's more like it," he said with a grin.

"Now. What brings you to the church on a cold and snowy Monday afternoon?"

Wendy frowned slightly and glanced about, trying to organize her thoughts. "I've got a question."

"OK."

"It's kinda serious."

The man nodded. "Then I'll do my best to give it a serious answer."

Wendy took in a deep breath and held it for a second or two. Then she let it out and spoke slowly, deliberately. "Are you still a Christian," she asked, "when you don't *feel* like one?"

Webley's eyebrows rose just a little.

"Know what I mean?" the girl continued. "Sometimes I know what I should do, and I even do it because I'm supposed to. But I don't *feel* like doing it. What I really want to do is punch someone right in the nose."

Pastor Webley suppressed an unexpected grin. Then he studied his hands for a long moment before speaking. "Little lady," he said, "you've stumbled upon a problem that every Christian faces at one time or another."

"Even you?" Wendy gasped.

The man nodded. "The apostle Paul got all tongue twisted one day trying to explain that the things he wanted to do he didn't do and the things he didn't want to do he did. He finally gave up and moaned, 'What a wretched man I am! Who will deliver me from this body of sin?'" Pastor Webley thought for a moment. "Yes, I must admit that I've sat in meetings when it was all I could do not to stand up and tell a church member what I *really* thought about his or her actions. I just wanted to grab 'em by the shoulders and shake some sense into 'em."

The girl's eyes widened. "So, whad'ya do?"

"I smiled and nodded my head and said something like, 'You know, my good brother or my good sister, I see that you feel very strongly about this matter, that it's important to you. So I'm going to give you my undivided attention until we figure out how to resolve this situation.' Then I go home and mow the lawn . . . twice!"

A grin spread across Wendy's face. "Yeah. Or you ride your horse way up into the mountains and race across the high meadows and yell at Mount Blackmore until your throat hurts."

The pastor blinked. "Wow! I see you've come up with a stress-reducer of your own. 'Course, the best thing for any Christian is not to get upset in the first place. That's where you've gotta work the hardest. Gettin' mad is easy. *Not* gettin' mad takes real determination and guts."

Wendy sighed. "I know what you mean. I don't like feeling angry. And I don't like wanting to punch someone out. But sometimes things happen and *bang,* I'm all tensed up inside and just wanna explode." She paused. "So does Jesus still love me when I get that way?"

The minister smiled. "If He didn't, we'd all be in a lot of trouble. There'd be no hope for us because we've got thousands of years of sin in our bones, thousands of years of ancestors who've passed down to us bad habits and evil tendencies. Problem is we're sin-weakened human beings, vulnerable to anger and lust and selfishness and a whole bunch of other nasty stuff. But God knows that. After all, Jesus was a human being once. He learned first-hand what it's like to feel like we feel."

"So what're we supposed to do?" Wendy asked, leaning forward in her chair.

"We're supposed to mow lawns and ride horses and shout at mountains until we learn how to handle our frustrations in more constructive ways."

"What ways?"

Pastor Webley reached over and picked up the crown made out of thorns resting on a nearby shelf. He held it in his hands for a long moment. "Do you know what killed Jesus?"

Wendy shrugged. "Sin?"

"Nope. Sin may have put Him on the cross. Sin may have made the people laugh at Him and spit on Him and drive nails through His hands. But that's not what killed Him. It was love—love for us imperfect, angry, unforgiving, selfish human beings. That's what made Him do it. That's what drove Him to that spot outside of Jerusalem where shouting mobs tortured the life right out of Him. Jesus turned His frustration and anger into something wonderful—sacrifice. He allowed Himself to be crucified so that He could earn the right to stand by our sides when we feel angry and offer help, support, and strength as we fight to overcome our feelings." The minister paused. "So let me ask you a question, Wendy. What makes you a Christian? Your feelings? Or is it realizing why Jesus died and then allowing Him to help you deal constructively with your feelings?"

Wendy sat in silence for a moment as the harmonies from the distant organ drifted in through the open door. What Pastor Webley had said made sense. It meant that even when she was facing the likes of Garwin Huffinger, even when she was working hard to control her anger, she was being loved by the same God that she felt so far away from at that particular moment. Jesus had died for angry people. He had died for her.

The girl nodded slowly. "I understand," she said quietly. "And I think it's neat."

Pastor Webley smiled. "Yeah. It is neat, isn't it?"

Joey looked up to see Wendy walking into the sanctuary. He watched her head for the front of the room and look for a long time at the big wooden cross hanging behind the podium. Then she turned. "We can go now," she said.

The boy stood and waved at Mrs. Webley, who returned his farewell with one hand while continuing to play with the other. As the two young people buckled themselves into the truck and Joey was pumping the accelerator in preparation for starting the engine, Wendy said, "Do you know what?"

"What?"

"I don't want to feel mad anymore."

Joey blinked. "OK."

"But," the girl continued, "if I do sometimes feel mad, I'm still a Christian."

Her companion nodded. "OK."

She glanced over at him. "So the next time you think I'm getting mad at you, just tell me to go and yell at Mount Blackmore."

"Mount Blackmore?" He stared at her in puzzlement.

"Yup."

He shrugged. "OK."

"Good."

Together they drove away, leaving behind the little church by the highway and the beautiful music filtering through its timbers and spilling out across the snows.

Fading afternoon shadows crept amid the cold snowdrifts piled against a little brick house on a back street in Bozeman. Winter chill had chased all the children who lived on the street into homes where warm soup waited and televisions heralded the evening news from living rooms and dens.

Frost-tinted windowpanes framed images of laughter and contentment, creating crystalline mosaics of life in a small western town set within the foothills of the Gallatin National Forest. However, one of the images was unlike the others. Beyond this particular wooden window frame sat a young girl, face damp with tears. She rested at the end of her bed, head bowed forward as if the very weight of it was more than she could bear. Her hands lay motionless in her lap, and her quiet sobs carried within their fabric the rough texture of a breaking heart.

Across the room sat a large cardboard box, its lid open to reveal a male mallard duck standing straight and tall, flapping its wings again and again as if the animal were rehearsing the movements of a dance he would soon perform. The brush of stiff feathers, the power of the wind being swept aside by their rhythmic motion, the *flap, flap, flap* of the exuberant exercise filled the small room with sound.

It was a familiar ritual in nature, a common spectacle seen beside a thousand lakes and rivers across the North Country. For centuries, ducks had performed this dance as they prepared to follow some unseen, unheard directive buried deep in the cortex of their brains. The animal didn't know why he stood in the box flapping his wings again and again and again. He just knew he should, that for some reason it was important, necessary, even vital.

Emily closed her eyes as if to shut out a sight

she'd never seen before. She understood the dance, knew what it meant and how quickly it could leave her without the friend she'd come to love during that past week. Into her world had fallen a true kindred spirit, a creature just like her, unable to fly, unable to soar away from the dangers and sadness of life. Now that same friend was listening to another voice, another summons that all nature hears.

The girl allowed her gaze to lift to the box. She saw the proud head of the duck rising above the rim, its eyes clear and focused, its body gaining strength and vibrancy.

As the last remnants of the day faded beyond the windowpane, as the room settled into darkness, Emily spoke, her words riding the rough edges of her breath. "Feathers, please, don't go. Please don't go."

Up and down the street a cold wind moaned as if sharing her sorrow—and her fear.

"Wendy Hanson, may I speak to you in my office?" The registrar glared down at the girl as she gathered her books from her locker.

"Yes, ma'am," Wendy responded politely. "I think Miss Elrod will let me leave math class a little earl—"

"Now."

"Now's good," Wendy nodded.

The two walked quickly through the crowd of students to the big office by the front entrance. Wendy soon found herself standing before the school official whose face stared back at her with a dark, stony expression. The girl decided that it looked just like some great and terrible monster had grabbed the registrar and sucked all the humanity right out of her.

"What did you want to see me about?" Wendy asked, trying to sound cheerful.

The woman didn't answer. She just picked up a pile of papers and dropped them with a quiet *splat* on the counter separating them. The first line on the first page of the first form contained a familiar name. "Feathers."

"Are you aware," the registrar began, her words as cold as the snow clinging to the windows by the file cabinets, "that I registered into the Lewis and Clark Elementary School a duck? That I placed him in first grade? That I gave him a meal ticket and a box of pencils? That I provided precise instructions on how he can have his picture included in our fine, award-winning yearbook? Has any of this come to your attention at all?"

Wendy was about to answer when she noticed a certain look in the registrar's eyes. She stared at the woman for a long time, trying to make sure she was reading the situation correctly. Finally, she answered, "I can't imagine you doing anything like that, ma'am."

The woman nodded. "Good."

With that she picked up the pile of forms, letters, and grade-report sheets and dropped them with a muffled *thud* into the large plastic trash can by her legs. "Now," she said, "I think you'd better hurry off to class. I've got work to do."

Wendy turned and walked to the door. Before leaving, she stopped and smiled back at the registrar. "Ma'am?"

"Yes?"

"You have a nice day, OK?"

The woman smiled ever so slightly. "I will."

With a nod Wendy exited the room, closing the door quietly behind her.

The last bell rang just as she reached the classroom. Students hurried to their desks and settled in quickly, preparing to discover even more fascinating facts about South America. As Wendy took her seat she glanced over at Emily's desk. It was empty. So was the spot where Feather's box usually rested by the bookcase.

H'mm, the girl thought to herself. *She musta missed the bus. Guess I'd better call her during the first break to make sure everything's OK.* Wendy realized there was actually no cause for real concern. Emily had told her that she missed a lot of classes while visiting clinics for tests, going to different hospitals for examination, or simply fighting the potential of a common cold by staying in bed for a day or two.

But try as she might, Wendy just couldn't concentrate on her studies. She kept remembering the look on Emily's face the day before as they had hurried to leave the school. Desperation had lurked in her smile, an uncomfortableness in the way she was acting as she climbed the steps of the bus and waved goodbye from the window. Something was happening to Emily, and Wendy wasn't quite sure what it was.

"Miss Elrod?"

The teacher looked up from her grade book. "Yes, Wendy?" the woman responded with a kind smile.

"I . . . ah . . . I need to make a phone call."

"Who to?"

Wendy motioned toward the empty desk in the center of the room. "Emily," she said. "I'm a little worried about her. She was kinda down yesterday, and now she's not here today."

Her teacher frowned. "Should we be concerned?"

The girl shrugged. "I don't know. If it's OK, I'd just like to call her so I can see if she's home and stuff. May I?"

"Yes. By all means. Why don't you go down to the nurse's office. That way you'll have someone nearby if you need help with Emily."

"Great. I'll be right back."

Hurrying from the classroom, Wendy ran down

the empty corridor leading to the office of the pretty nurse she'd met the week before. After explaining the reason for her visit, she dialed the number Emily had scribbled on a scrap of paper before the weekend. She heard the phone ring three times, then a weak voice answered.

"Emily?" Wendy said, "are you OK?"

A long pause. "I'm OK."

"Why didn't you come to school?"

"I . . . I didn't want to."

"Why?"

No answer.

"Is Feathers OK? Did you give him a big breakfast?"

"I tried to."

Wendy frowned. "So, do you need anything—any medicine or stuff?"

"No."

Wendy glanced at the nurse, then at the oxygen bottle resting in the corner of the room. Something in the way Emily talked, in the way she breathed, worried her, made her feel extremely uneasy. "Listen, Emily, I'd like to come to your house if it's all right."

"You don't have to."

"I know. But you sound kinda sad and . . . and I just want to talk to you. I won't stay very long if you don't want me to."

"Sure. Do whatever you like. I don't care."

Wendy's eyes narrowed as a feeling of fear rose

in her throat. "I'll be there soon. I gotta tell you what happened this morning at the registrar's office. You're gonna love it."

"Fine. Whatever."

The phone went dead. Wendy paused for only a second before quickly dialing another number. When an adult voice answered, she said, "Miss Cadena please." Pressing the receiver closer to her ear she added, "Hurry. This is an emergency."

The newly plowed street seemed deserted as the social worker's car slowed and headed for the curb fronting a small brick house near the corner. Wendy was out the door even before Miss Cadena brought her vehicle to a complete stop. The girl raced up the sidewalk, boots crunching in the hard-packed snow. At the door, she pressed the bell and waited, stabbed the button again, and then again. "Emily? Emily?"

Nothing.

Glancing back at Ruth Cadena who was walking quickly up the driveway, she ran around to the side of the little dwelling. "Emily? It's Wendy. Can you hear me?"

Stopping at a low window, she peered inside. She could just make out a threadbare couch and end table. Continuing around to the back door she began pounding on the wooden frame. "Emily. It's Wendy. Open up. Let me in."

Miss Cadena joined her on the small porch and added her knock to the pounding. They stopped when they heard the latch rattle. Then the door opened a crack. "Why are you here?" a tired voice breathed.

"Emily. Open the door, please," Wendy called. "I just want to talk to you, that's all. Open the door so we can come in. Miss Cadena came with me. We're worried about you."

"Yes, Emily," the woman called, "we were thinking you'd like another visit to the mountains. What do you think? Up for a wagon ride with Joey?"

The door slowly opened to reveal a girl who looked as if she hadn't slept for a long time. "I . . . I can't."

"Why not?"

"I gotta go away."

Wendy pressed in close to her friend. "Go away where?"

Turning, Emily walked slowly into the kitchen. "My mom and dad told me this morning. We're moving to Chicago, to some big hospital where they can treat my disease better—at least that's what they say." She glanced back at her friends. "I don't want to go. I want to stay here in Montana."

Ruth Cadena nodded slowly as Wendy stepped forward. "Oh, Emily, I'm sorry. But, after you get well, you can come back. Then we can—"

"No," Emily interrupted, looking down at the floor. "You don't understand. I . . . I won't be coming back. Not ever."

Wendy's breath caught in her throat. Suddenly

she couldn't speak, couldn't think. All she could do was stare at the gaunt, ashen face of her friend, trying to fathom the full meaning of Emily's words. She wanted to scream, to shout out her defiance to the news she'd just heard. It couldn't be true—it just couldn't. Her friend was sick, that was all. And sick people got well. They eventually crawled out of bed and wandered around coughing and sneezing, perhaps even limping on injured limbs for a while, but they didn't go to Chicago and never come back again. That wasn't right—that wasn't fair!

It was Emily who broke the silence. "Feathers can fly now," she said. "He can fly south, because he's all better."

Wendy nodded.

"So," the girl continued, "I think we should take him outside and let him go. It's the right thing to do."

Miss Cadena stepped forward. "It's OK, Emily. We can wait a few more days."

"No. That's the worst thing—keeping an animal from doing what it wants. Feathers doesn't belong here—doesn't belong in a box. He should be out there, high in the sky, flying to his family, to their pond far away from here." Motioning toward the cardboard box in the narrow hallway leading to her bedroom, she said, "I tried to give him a big breakfast, lots of lettuce and stuff, but he just flapped his wings and looked at me as if he was saying, 'Why don't you let me go? Why are you keeping me here?'" Emily wiped a tear from her cheek with a trembling hand. "So let's just take him outside so he can do what he wants to do."

Wendy glanced over at Miss Cadena, then shook her head slowly. "It wasn't supposed to be like this," she said to her friend. "You were *both* supposed to get well."

"I know," Emily stated. "But sometimes bad things happen even on a planet of joy. Isn't that what Pastor Webley said?"

Closing her eyes tightly, Wendy fought to control her emotions. "I'm sorry," she whispered. "I'm so very sorry, Emily."

The girls wrapped their arms around each other, crying softly, holding onto each other tightly, unable to find the words to describe the feelings that burned in their hearts. They'd come into each other's worlds riding the injured wings of a wild animal. Now they were about to watch those same wings, grown stronger, fly away, leaving behind the stark reality that not all stories have a happy ending.

Miss Cadena picked up the box and together the three made their way through the house and out the front door. The yard and street were empty, completely devoid of cars and people. In the distance, past the leafless trees, beyond the low roofs of the houses, rose distant mountains, their summits white and glistening in the morning sun.

The social worker placed the box on the snow-covered sidewalk and looked over at her companions. "Just take off the blanket," Emily said. "He'll know what to do."

Wordlessly, Miss Cadena bent and slipped the cover off the container. Immediately, Feather's head popped up above the rim and he looked around, a little confused. For a moment he studied the thin branches high overhead, then glanced back at the girls. "It's OK," Emily called softly. "You can go now. It's what you want to do. It's what you have to do."

The bird hesitated, still unsure of what was happening. For a solid week he'd been at the mercy of human hands, allowing them to bring him food and offer comfort as his body healed. Now those hands remained at a distance. No smiling face hovered over him. No soothing voice called his name and spoke sounds that calmed his racing heart.

Suddenly, the mallard turned as if hearing a distant call from somewhere far away. This voice he understood. It spoke his language, inviting him to rise above the earth and seek the horizon, to leave the hands to which he'd become accustomed and fly free, following his own thoughts, going his own way.

The duck's head began to bob up and down in short, quick movements as he became nervous, excited, even fearful. He didn't belong in a box, didn't need human hands to care for him. Instead, he was a wild animal, a creation of nature, a feathered spirit made to race the winds that streamed south, away from the cold and the mountains and the presence of people.

With powerful flaps of his wings, he rose quickly from the box like a ball shot from a cannon, and raced away, skimming over the snow, gaining speed and confidence, feeling the rush of icy air as it whistled past his beak and eyes and outstretched neck. Up he flew, watching the earth drop away, feeling a familiar urgency drive his every bone, muscle, and feather. He was going to some distant place far to the south. Although he didn't know where or why, he just knew he had to go there. And the mountains, the glorious mountains, would lead him home.

The long winter was just beginning to lose its grip on the land as Wendy walked the distance from the Station to the end of the driveway. She breathed in the crisp air, squinting into the brilliant sky, trying to imagine what the world would look like without the blanket of snow that had covered the valleys for so many months.

When she reached the road, she sat down on a worn wooden bench jutting from the drifts and waited. It wouldn't be long now, if he kept to his schedule.

The girl glanced back at the Station and admired the proud, handsome structure nestled among the sparse pines and open pastures. Early and the other members of the ranch herd stomped about under the cottonwoods, exploring the dead grasses just under the surface of the snow. They too were searching for hints that spring would soon return.

"Imagine finding you here," she heard someone call. Wendy turned to see Joey leading Tar Boy in from their afternoon jaunt on the logging roads above the valley. "Has he come yet?"

"Nope."

A little red minivan approached, following the road that led past the ranch and intersected the long driveway. The two immediately recognized the driver and his passenger and waved. When it reached them, the vehicle crunched to a stop.

"Has he come yet?"

"Nope."

Debbie slipped out of the van and made her way to the mailbox. "Someone needs to paint this thing," she commented.

Mr. Hanson joined her and nodded in agreement. "Sounds like a good job for our ranch's new, official, full-time head wrangler," he said, glancing at Joey.

"Like I told someone once, *everything's* in my job description," the young man said with a smile. "Even mailboxes. Now that Barry's buying and selling horses over the Internet like some kinda cyberwrangler, I guess all the odd jobs belong to me too. I'm such a lucky guy."

Mr. Hanson grinned. "Hey, you get to spend time with the likes of us plus you can have all the horse manure you can shovel."

Another vehicle approached, this one sporting a little yellow rotating light fastened to the top and a license plate that announced it belonged to the United States Postal Service.

"Hey, Mr. Goldstein," Wendy called as the smiling face of the courier stopped in front of her. "Anything for me?"

"Yeah, like there never is," he laughed, reaching beside him and withdrawing a handful of mail. "Enjoy. See you tomorrow."

With a wave, the man drove away, his little light flashing out a warning to whatever deer or wild animal it needed to of his approach.

Wendy grinned broadly as she selected an envelope addressed to her in firm handwritten letters. She passed the other correspondence to her father, who fished through it with enthusiasm. "Yup," he said, "here it is. A note from Mrs. Pierce. This should tell us what day to expect her and what flight she'll be coming in on. This is wonderful. We'll all be together again, just like before. Lizzy's sister's health is back to normal, and soon so will be Shadow Creek Ranch."

With a nod Wendy ripped open her letter. She read it through quickly, then sighed.

"Well?" Debbie said, "are you going to share it with us?"

Her younger sister nodded. "OK. But, I'll leave out the personal, girl-type stuff. Wouldn't want to embarrass Mr. Dugan. He's very sensitive, you know."

Joey nodded. "When it comes to some of the crazy things those two discuss, you're right."

Spreading the paper out on her lap, Wendy smoothed it with her gloved hand. "Dear Wendy," she began. "I really enjoyed your last letter. It made me homesick for Montana and especially the ranch. Every night I go to sleep imagining that I'm riding with you and Joey up in the mountains. It sometimes helps me forget how much my chest hurts and how lonely I am in this big hospital.

"The doctors say I'm doing a little better, but they're always whispering among themselves, which may or may not be a good sign. It really doesn't matter anymore. I'm learning to take one day at a time and not get too discouraged.

"Tell Pastor Webley 'thank you' for that book he sent to me in your Easter package. I've read it three times. It's all about heaven and stuff, and I really like to think about what it's going to be like to live there and run around with you and chase ducks who will never ever fly away.

"You know, I don't think I have to wait to start enjoying heaven. I can go there now in my mind and even in my dreams. Maybe that's what it's like to live in a planet of joy. Maybe that's what I need to do when I get to feeling sorry for myself.

"Well, the nurse with the crooked mouth just came in. She says I've got to get hooked up to some machine for an hour or two. It's supposed to help build up my good lung. Hey, who am I to argue with technology? So be good and WRITE ME AGAIN SOON. You're my best friend, Wendy. As a matter of fact, you're my *only* friend, but who's counting?

"Give Debbie and Wrangler Barry and Samantha and Joey and Grandpa and Grandma Hanson and your dad my love. Oh yes, and Miss Cadena too. I think it's really great that your dad finally asked that poor woman to marry him. She's been waiting forever!

"I love you, Wendy, and I think about you every day.

"Your friend, Emily."

Wendy looked up at her father with a grin. "I told her about you and Miss Cadena. Hope you don't mind."

Mr. Hanson laughed. "Fine with me. And I agree with Emily. I *did* wait far too long. Now I'm eager for June so we can have another wedding by the footbridge. You're all invited, by the way."

Debbie shook her head as she trudged back to the minivan. "I don't know. I might be doing something else that day—washing shirts or sewing on a new dress."

"Yeah," Joey added, picking up Tar Boy's reins

and guiding him toward the driveway. "I might have to miss it too. Gotta fix that weak place in the fence at the far end of the pasture."

Mr. Hanson looked at Wendy, his eyes filled with mock despair. "And you, my youngest and strangest daughter? Will you also abandon me on my day of bliss?"

Wendy shook her head. "Not a chance. I'll be there, Daddy. And for you, I might even put on that silly dress again. I'm not making any promises, you understand. But I'll think about it."

"Fair enough," he stated as he hopped into the van. "Now hurry home. We've gotta plan a welcome back party for Mrs. Pierce. And I think Grandma's making pancakes. Why she's making pancakes for supper is beyond me."

"Ah, that's my fault," Debbie said. "I asked her to. I've been having these weird cravings lately. Yesterday it was catsup and pickles. Is that gross or what?"

Mr. Hanson stared at his daughter for a long moment. "You gotta be kidding."

"What?" the girl blinked.

"You gotta be kidding!"

"Daddy, what's the matter with you? Can't a girl get hungry for catsup and pickles on this ranch?"

Wendy watched Joey and his horse trail the little red minivan with its laughing driver as it moved down the long driveway. The Station waited in the distance, rising from the snow like a friendly fort, its face pleasant and inviting. She folded the letter and slipped it into her pocket. "I miss you, Emily," she said quietly. "I really miss you."

With that she stood and began following the snow-covered pathway that led up the valley and ended at the steps of her home. Overhead, the mountains looked down on her, warming themselves in the breezes that now flowed from the south, bringing the promise of new life to the frozen land. She knew, as did all of nature, that winters never last forever. With the spring would come the excitement of rebirth and the rewards of fresh, unexpected challenges. Soon she'd glance skyward and see returning lines of ducks and geese. Once more there'd be wings filling the skies over Shadow Creek Ranch.